CAMPFIRE
ADVENTURE STORIES

Campfire: Adventures Stories

Copyright © 2024 by Peter Westerman

Published by Peter Westerman
   8 W Chestnut St, #11b
   Chicago, IL 60610

All rights reserved. No part of this publication may be reproduced, stored in a retrieval system, or transmitted in any form by any means, electronic, mechanical, photocopy, recording, or otherwise, without prior permission of the publisher, except as provided for by USA copyright law.

Cover Photo by Vlad Bagacian from Pexels

General Editing by Peter Westerman

Contributing Authors: Joseph Coughlin, Various Authors, Donald Smith (The Silver Orb), David White (Andy the Dragon Fighter), Peter Westerman (The Widow's Son)

Illustrations by Elizabeth Westerman

First printing 2020

ISBN: 9798432113849
Imprint: Independently published

Printed in the United States of America

This book is dedicated to

Joseph W. Coughlin, a master storyteller.

Joseph W. Coughlin, or "Uncle Joe," was the founder of Christian Service Brigade. His stories ignited the imagination of every audience. This book is filled with some of Joe's favorite stories along with some from those he inspired.

TABLE OF CONTENTS

Editor's Note	1
The Story of the Torch	3
Run of the Arrow	5
The Great Knight	9
My Son	13
The Great Strong One	15
Enough	21
City Without Water	25
A Slave Set Free	27
The Mountain Stream	31
The Man on the Cross	35
Where is the Christian?	41
El Capitan	45

The Lucky Stone	49
God's Garden	53
The Crowning of the King	63
Legend of the Cottonwoods	67
Forty Roman Wrestlers	71
The Blacksmith	73
Goldie	75
Goosetown	79
Sir Brian's Shield	81
Andy the Dragon Fighter	87
The Widow's Son	93
New Rags for Old	97
The Silver Orb	101
Appendix	107

    Themes and Key Verses
    Story Adaptations
    Learning a story
    Storytelling Techniques
    Best Practices
    A Story's End

CAMPFIRE

EDITOR'S NOTE

We are people of stories. God created us to enjoy telling stories and listen to those told by others. Through sharing we communicate passion, fear, joy and sadness. There's something almost magical about a well-told tale—it pulls us and makes our hearts pound, tears swell, and brings comfort.

The stories in this book have been told at thousands of campfires. I am not sure if anyone knows who told them first. Whoever created them would not recognize them as they exist on these pages. Every time a story is told, the teller changes it by making it their own. The story will never be the same again.

Think of the campfire—of the flickering, dancing flames. The fire is made from the same wood, but it burns differently. The flames flow, change direction, and take on a form of their own. Stories are like that fire–familiar but also unique. They draw people in and hold them together in warmth.

Campfire stories are for reading, for telling, and retelling. Use them the way you like them best, and as you pass the story and on to one another, remember you are part of a great campfire tradition.

CAMPFIRE

THE STORY OF THE TORCH

Long before there were telephones, airplanes, or overnight delivery, there was an efficient system for relaying messages through the Highlands of ancient Scotland. Each village had a torch runner, a brave and noble man who was able at any time of night or day to carry a message swiftly to the next town.

It was the responsibility of the runner to pass the torch and the message to the next runner, and then tell the news to the villagers. From one village to the next, the news traveled as quickly as the experienced runners could carry it.

One of the famed torchbearers had a son who was eager to follow in his father's footsteps. How that boy worshiped his father! He loved to run out from the village each time a new message went on its way to the next town. As the boy grew older and stronger, he could run a little farther before the torch's flickering light disappeared through the night. At last, he could run all the way with his father, and they walked back together after the message was delivered. At his father's side, he learned every inch of the way.

One day, the boy's father grew very ill. On that very night, a runner arrived with an urgent message to be carried to the next town. Who would take the torch? Who would deliver the message? As the villagers stood helpless and speechless, the young man seized the torch, read the message, and set out through the darkness for the village beyond.

THE STORY OF THE TORCH

Because he had seen the need and boldly jumped into the gap, his name became well-known throughout the land.

But in that same country, there lived another torch runner. It was his task to carry the message from his town on the mainland to a small village at the end of a point that jutted far out into the sea. It was a long, hard journey to that village. There were many hills, rocks, and paths. But he was considered a robust and brave runner.

One night, after his energy was spent in hours of hard work, he heard a loud banging on the door just as he was drifting off to sleep. The flickering light of the torch outside told him there was a message to be carried to the distant point.

He quickly dressed and hurried out. Listening briefly to the news, he took the torch and was off into the darkness. Just as he was out of sight, his feet began to feel very heavy, and he could hardly lift them.

Then, suddenly, he thought of his friend, the torch runner in the village on the other side of the narrow neck of land, a short distance away. If he ran across to this town instead of going out to that little village on the point, no one would know. The torch would continue its journey to the other towns.

So, he ran across the shorter distance and gave the message to his friend. It went on around the circuit, and all the villages of Scotland heard the news of an approaching enemy—except one.

That night the enemy came from the northern sea. The first place they struck was that one little village which jutted out into the sea. Because the people there were sleeping and did not get the message, the enemy could conquer them and do extensive damage in all the land.

CAMPFIRE

RUN OF THE ARROW

Two young Indian boys were preparing for their final and most challenging test of manhood by running up a long hill. It was a steep climb, but not nearly as difficult as the Mountain of Two Suns would be.

The boys were Running Deer and White Fox, and on the day following the next full moon, they would begin their final test of manhood—the Run of the Arrow. The boys had completed many tests before. They had tracked a mountain lion through hard-packed clay, captured and trained wild ponies, and made hunting boys to name a few. The Run of the Arrow, however, was the toughest test. It was survival under challenging conditions.

As the boys ran together, they discussed what would happen if one of them got injured during the Run of the Arrow. Running Deer assured White Fox that they could outsmart the enemy if they helped the injured boy.

The Run of the Arrow combined the hunting and tracking skills required for the boys to overcome the challenge of a proven enemy. The test began by having a Indian brave, Black Stag, shoot an arrow with his bow. Then, the boys would start the run from the point where the arrow landed while Black Stag pursued them. They had a two-day journey to the top of the Mountain of Two suns. If either boy was caught by Black Stag or failed to complete the run, he would be denied the chance to become a brave.

RUN OF THE ARROW

White Fox and Running Deer got up before sunrise to make their final preparations, such as putting enough food in their leather pouches to get nourishment along the way.

The starting line for the run was just outside the village and all the men, including the proven braves, followed the boys out to see the start. The boys wanted so badly to be like those men—proven braves.

The chief broke an arrow to start the race. The brave chosen to pursue the boys, Black Stag, shot his arrow far and high, hundreds of yards over dense, low brush. The boys moved to take their position where the arrow landed. A smoke signal went up and the race began, with the Mountain of Two Suns miles away. Running Deer and White Fox started off in a low, measured run, dodging through bushes. Sometimes they crawled to keep from being seen, but they always kept moving. Their movements were quick, but they didn't stop because they knew they had a long way to go.

After an hour, they broke through a long clearing. They ran hard through the clearing because they desired at all times to remain undercover. Their breathing was long and deep but not panting. Many months of conditioning had gone into preparation for this run.

After several miles, they approached the foothills of the Mountain of Two Suns. They felt the sun getting hotter and they slowed to a walk in the heat of the day. Stopping occasionally to drink or eat lightly. As dusk approached, they looked for a place to hide and spend the night. There was no sign of Black Stag yet, but they were quiet, talking only in low tones.

The boys again discussed what would happen if one of them should get hurt. Would one stop to help the other and risk being caught, or would one go on and make sure he made it to the end of the run, leaving the other to be caught? They said they would stay and help the other, but inside they both knew they couldn't be sure until the situation occurred.

White Fox and Running Deer were up before the sun again and grabbed a quick bite to eat. At sunup, they could see the reflection from the Mountain of Two Suns. It reminded them of the heat they would bear later in the afternoon. During the afternoon, while drinking from a spring, they spotted Black Stag. They were startled, but he didn't see them. They were still two miles from the Mountain of Two Suns, and they decided to make one final dash for the top. As they climbed, the ground got rockier, the going got tougher, the sun got hotter, and they got more and more tired.

As the boys continued running up the steep incline, White Fox slipped, fell back, and broke his ankle. Running Deer turned to see what had happened and, at the

CAMPFIRE

same time, spotted Black Stag beginning to climb the mountain. This was it. He must decide either to help White Fox or to continue his climb, realizing that his friend White Fox would not become a brave. Running Deer thought for a moment and went back to help White Fox. He started to splint the ankle and explained a plan for them to both reach the top. White Fox refused the help and urged Running Deer to go for the top. Running Deer tried to explain the plan, but White Fox insisted he leave. Finally, Running Deer agreed. White Fox had made his decision, and now he must live with it for the rest of his life. Running Deer headed for the top and, a few minutes later, Black Stag arrived and plucked the feathers from White Fox's headband, signifying his failure. Meanwhile, Running Deer continued up and reached the top.

White Fox refused Running Deer's help even though Running Deer tried his best to help him. Running Deer tried several times to save White Fox. White Fox had all the help he needed there, but he refused it. He never had another chance.

"With great joy and all the courage he was famous for, the Great Knight rode forth and, with great humility and powerful words, turned the people from the path of destruction...and the land was once again filled with harmony and plenty."

CAMPFIRE

THE GREAT KNIGHT

Many years ago, there was a land ruled by a wise and good King. The King had taught the people in his kingdom to respect what was good and to help one another in word and deed. The words integrity, honor, loyalty, and compassion were alive in this place. It was a land of harmony and plenty.

Also, in the land was the Great Knight. The Great Knight received his title from the King himself for his courage and strength in battle. The people spoke highly of him and even praised him to his face—recounting his great exploits in the King's service.

Because of all this attention, the Great Knight's thoughts become more and more boastful. He spent much of his time thinking of his successes and planning ways to make the people talk about him even more.

He began to share these thoughts with his squire. The squire listened respectfully, but each time said, "You have been greatly blessed by the King! All praise to the King!"

This angered the Great Knight. He took his stories to the village squares where the people listened intently and said, "How magnificent you are—so full of bravery and strength!" Then the Great Knight would hold his head high, laugh loudly, and boast of things he planned to do.

One day, as he approached the village square, he overheard one of the

THE GREAT KNIGHT

townspeople speaking of the heroic adventures of another knight—Sir Tremont. As he listened, the man ended his story with the words, "He may even be as brave as the Great Knight."

The Great Knight's heart sank. He did not go into the village that day, but returned home and sat all day with his thoughts. Toward evening he decided that the next day he must return to the square and prove to the people that he was indeed the Great Knight—and not by accident. "I must tell of my greatest victories," he said to himself, "and perhaps even a few of Sir Tremont's flaws," he chuckled.

The next day he did just that—but he didn't stop at only Sir Tremont's flaws. He began to make fun of and tell embarrassing stories about all the other knights, as well. The townspeople laughed so hard at the stories that he continued them for some time.

Later on, the other knights heard about all this and were surprised and upset. They gather together to decide what they should do. Finally, having decided that the King must know, they set off as a group to the castle.

When the King heard what had happened, and had proved with other witnesses that it was so, he was grieved. He sent word to the Great Knight to come to him at once.

Immediately upon receiving the message, the Great Knight came to the King expecting to be given some great deed of valor to perform or some honor to receive as had happened so often before. But quickly his smile turned to a look of astonishment as the King removed from his armor the seal of the Great Knight.

"You have disgraced this land and my service," said the King, "and you have hurt me deeply. You are no longer the Great Knight. Alas, there is no one in all the land to match your skill and bravery in battle, but you will not be called to my service until you can see the harm you have done. Now depart from here and study your heart."

The Great Knight slinked away from the castle hiding his face in shame—but there was another feeling inside him, too—anger! "Does not the King remember who I am?" he railed, "and how I earned my title from him?! I have fought many battles and brought great victories for the King by my own hand. Does he not remember these? I have been better to him than all his other knights combined! He must be crazy to send me away like this. Just wait. As soon as the kingdom is attacked, he will call on me as before and restore me to his service. If he is lucky, perhaps I will accept his meager invitation—if he is lucky!"

Indeed, in a nearby country, an evil King was plotting to attack the good King's land. The evil King brought together all the forces of his mighty army and marched against the good King.

CAMPFIRE

The Great Knight heard of it and said to himself, "Now the King will come to me and beg me to return. Ha, ha! I shall make him worry for a time and then return in honor and lead the army to victory." But no invitation came. Instead, the King gathered his faithful knights of lesser ability around him and told them that he would lead them into the battle. All the knights gave a mighty cheer and, with great excitement and determination, rode out to engage the enemy.

The battle was short. The good King's knights, carefully following their lord's directions, overpowered the evil King's army and sent them scurrying back to their own country. Then they returned to the castle with great joy in their hearts! The celebration was long and loud!

The Great Knight heard it and decided to sneak up toward the castle to find out what had happened. He hid behind a corner and listened to the many conversations. One spoke of his own bravery that day and how he had killed more of the enemy than any other knight. Another said that the only reason the first was able to kill so many was because the second had fended off a whole group with his magnificent swordplay. The Great Knight was aghast when he heard one say that they really didn't need the King with them—that the outcome had been certain because of their own abilities. But one conversation especially caught his ear. It was about him!—the Great Knight! The people were making fun of his disgrace and began to talk about the mistakes he had made over the years! First, it was just one man speaking, but then more joined in. "Why do they not talk about my great victory at Kinsman Hill or of my great skill with the javelin? My skills are many, yet they speak only of my weaknesses and my mistakes!"

The Great Knight was dumbfounded, and, hiding in the shadows, ran back to his room. How could he ever show his face in the land again!

His squire saw his great distress and gently approached him. "My lord," began the squire, "you have many great skills and have received honor for them time and time again."

"Why is it, then, that the people remember only my failures?" asked the Great Knight.

The squire paused for a long time—not sure he wanted to say what he knew was the truth. Finally, he looked up and spoke, "My lord, perhaps it is because they look up to you so."

"Look up to me?" shouted the Great Knight. "How could they possibly talk about me in those ways if they looked up to me?"

"My lord," replied the squire, "from your youth you have been respected by all the people—especially the young men who want to be warriors in service to the King. They have watched your every move and tried to be just like you. They

THE GREAT KNIGHT

purchase the same kind of sword they see you have, wear a crest on their helmets as you do, and practice the javelin throw to be just like you."

"How is it, then, that they want to hurt me so with their words?" cried the Great Knight.

Again, the squire paused. Then, he spoke, "They speak these things, also, because they want to be just like you. Many times they have heard you speak of the other knights in the same way that they now speak about you. They are only doing what you taught them to do."

"Could this be so?" gasped the Great Knight. "If it is true, then I have done a great disservice to the King and all the people. If this manner of speech spreads, everyone in the land will feel useless and miserable as I do and we will be like all the other lands—full of hatred, strife and evil! I must see the King at once and work to save the kingdom!"

The Great Knight raced to the castle to seek an audience with the King. When it was granted, he bowed low before his Sovereign and said, "My lord, I ask your forgiveness for my selfish and foolish acts. I have been pierced by the same spear I hurled and so have seen my grave mistake. If others follow my error, our great land will suffer terrible loss and inner pain. Sire, if you allow it, I will put myself at your disposal to correct what I have done."

The King looked at the Great Knight for a long moment, then smiled broadly and said, "It is good to have you back. You are once again the Great Knight - but even greater than before, having learned this most important lesson. I accept you into my royal service to correct this grievous wrong and save the land. With the power I grant, you will succeed. Go now, and, at my bidding, rid the land of this evil."

With great joy and all the courage he was famous for, the Great Knight rode forth and, with great humility and powerful words, turned the people from the path of destructionand the land was once again filled with harmony and plenty.

CAMPFIRE

MY SON

This is the story of a wealthy, successful, caring man and his love for his only son. This was a powerful man—he was on the board of directors of many large corporations all over the world. He owned many large and beautiful homes in many countries. Yet, the man's most outstanding quality was his love and devotion to his son.

This love and devotion were never more evident than during his son's long battle with a severe illness. The man arranged for the best doctors, nurses, and care for his son, but despite all these efforts, the son could not overcome the illness and died.

Although the father was full of sorrow, he continued to live a happy, active, Christian life. He could rejoice in knowing his son was with the Lord.

The house where his son had lived was large and beautiful—like a mansion. It had costly furnishings. After the son's death, the father left the house just as before the boy died. Nothing was changed.

Years later, the father also died. His lawyers were faced with the problem of settling the man's estate. The man had kept accurate records of all his accounts. It appeared he had taken care of every detail, large and small. The man had left written instructions for the lawyers to follow. He had thought of everything. But there was one problem—there was no will. This puzzled the lawyers because the man had been so complete and precise in his instructions. How could he forget the will? The lawyers decided to simply follow the written instructions one step at a time.

Step one was to sell all the furnishings in the son's house. Everything was to be put up for sale in an auction that was to be run by a famous auctioneer that was specifically chosen by the father. Arrangements were made for the auction. It was heavily advertised and people came from all over to bid on the items.

Among the people attending the auction was one of the nurses who had cared for the boy while he was sick. She grew to love him as she took care of him every day. She still had this love in her heart and she wanted to buy a picture of him that was hanging on his bedroom wall. The nurse was older now and things had not gone too well for her lately. She was poor. She had brought only two dollars to auction and was afraid it wouldn't be enough to buy the portrait. She prayed ahead of time and even prayed at the auction that no one would outbid her for the picture. It seemed like forever to the old nurse as she clutched the two dollars in her hand and followed the auctioneer and crowd from room to room. People were eagerly buying expensive items of furniture.

Finally, they came to the son's bedroom. The furniture sold quickly. At last, the auctioneer pointed to the son's portrait hanging on the wall. The auctioneer asked for an opening bid on the picture. The nurse responded, "I'll bid everything I have, and that's two dollars."

There was silence. It seemed like forever, then the auctioneer said, "I have two dollars. Do I hear more? Going, going, gone. Sold for two dollars."

Quickly the nurse paid and rushed to the wall to get the picture of the boy she had so dearly loved. As she took the picture down, something fell from it. Surprised, she picked it up. It was an envelope with papers in it. She gave it to the auctioneer. He was puzzled and he gave it to the lawyers, saying it looked like a will. Sure enough, it was the missing will! Everyone held their breath as a lawyer read the will, "To the one who loved my son enough to want his portrait, I will all of my houses, all of my possessions and all of my money." The nurse inherited everything from the father because she loved the son.

CAMPFIRE

THE GREAT STRONG ONE

On the shores of a long narrow lake, surrounded by the virgin forests of the old Northwest, a man sat beside his campfire. In his lap opened before him, the Word of God. As the hour of twilight came, and great, long fingers of sunlight stretched out across the sky in brilliant colors of rose, orange, scarlet, and gold, he listened to the musical sound of the Indian evening call.

"Ya-a-a-ah Ha-a-ah we-e-e-e hay-y o-o-oh."

Then, from across the long, narrow lake by the shore of which he was seated, came the answer of the tribesmen.

"Ya-a-a-ah Ha-a-ah we-e-e-e hay-y o-o-oh."

Then back came the echo from the great sandstone cliff at the far end of the lake.

" Ya-a-a-ah Ha-a-ah we-e-e-e hay-y o-o-oh."

As the last sounds of the Indian evening call reverberated and died, and as the last brilliantly colored ray of the sunlight disappeared in the west, there was a motion among the sapling fir trees that encircled the spot where the man sat by his campfire. The boughs parted and an Indian entered.

The Indian was tall. His bronzed forehead was high and noble. He was a chieftain of the tribe. Raising his right hand in a sign of peace, he saluted the man of God in silence. The other, having stood to his feet to receive him, returned the sign of peace. No word was spoken. Both men stood near the campfire, watching the dancing flames listening to the crackle of the fire. At length it was the Indian who broke the silence,

"White man, tell Indian chief about white man's God."

Then welled up in the heart of the missionary praise to God for this opportunity long sought, now provided by His grace. Looking out across the long blue lake, he began,

"You know the lake and all the people of the lake—the fish, the beaver, the otter, and all the creatures that dwell in the lake. All of them move according to the will of God, live and die according to the Word that God speaks. All belong to God because he made them. He is the God of the lake."

The Indian chief gazed out across the long lake, and then, turning to his host, he nodded and spoke slowly, "The God of the lake? Yes, the God of the lake."

Then stretching his hand out toward the forest, the man of God continued. "Well do you know the forest, and all the people of the forest— the deer, the fox, the wolf—the wild creatures of the woodlands, great and small. All of them move, find their substance, live, give birth, and die according to God's will and plan. They are God's for He made them. He is the God of the forest."

After a moment of silence, the Indian chief answered, "Yes, the God of the forest... the God of the forest."

The missionary stretched out his arm in the direction of the great wide plain. "Well you know the prairies and all the people of the prairie who dwell on the surface of the plain—the antelope, the bison, and all that moves on the face of the prairie. All move, live, and have their being according to God's will, for He made them. They are His, for He is the God of the plain—the God of the prairie."

The tall Indian listened in silence and then, nodding his head imperceptibly, repeated the words, "Yes, the God of the prairie."

Stretching both arms above him into the great, sparkling, diamond-studded abyss of the skies, the man of God continued, "Well do you know the skies, the heavens, the people of the skies, the stars, the planets, the constellations and all that moves in the skies—all move according to the will of God. They are His because He has made them. He has ordered their course in the heavens, for He is the God of the heavens—the God of the skies."

Looking up into the sky in awe, the Indian chieftain spoke, a tone of wonder in his voice, "Yes, the God of the skies as well."

The missionary continued. "You know man—the red man, the white man—all men were made by God. He has ordered our ways. He has given us life. He has made us. The God of the lake, of the forest, of the plains, and of the heavens is the God of man as well—the red man, the white man—of every man on the face of the earth. There is but one God."

"The people of the lake, the people of the forest, the people of the plain, the people of the sky, the fish, the beasts, and the very stars move in accordance to God's will and obey Him. Of all His creatures, only man does not move in accordance to God's bidding, does not live according to God's will, but rather is disobedient, rebellious against Him. Man was made by God, but man has become God's enemy by his own desire. Man seeks to do the thing that is against God's will, and instead of seeking Him, he seeks to flee from His presence. Man is fleeing from God."

Well did the Indian know the ways of His people. Well did he know of the fighting that would go on among the men and women of his village. Well did he know the wickedness of the heart of man. The men of his village were prone to seek the warpath, to go to rob and kill. He nodded his head slowly and said, "Yes, man is God's enemy."

Then the missionary began to explain to the forest dweller the great and glorious story of God's grace. God had an only Son and sent Him to the earth as a man to suffer and to die so that man, who was His enemy, would become His friend.

When he heard these words, the Indian chief looked up in amazement, his eyes wide with wonder. How could such a thing be? Would not God destroy man rather than save him?

As much as he tried, the missionary could not explain to the Indian how God's love went far beyond the sin and rebellion of man. He sought in every way that he knew to explain that God is so gracious that He is willing to forgive man's sin, and was willing to make the great sacrifice of sending His own Son to suffer and die so that men might be brought back to friendship with God, instead of enmity against God.

But everything was without avail. The Indian persisted in saying, "Indian chief no understand. Man, God's enemy. God destroy man." At length the two lapsed into silence.

It was autumn in the great north woods. The tall maples and oaks discarded their summer verdure to display their brilliant leafy banners of yellow, red, gold, scarlet, and crimson. Then these colors had faded into the brown of late autumn. And these leaves had fallen, leaving great stark skeletons stretching against the autumn sky. The chill autumn breezes had spread the brown carpet of dried leaves over the floor of the forest.

The missionary, reaching out with a stick, made a great circle in the leaves, not far from the fire, and the keen, observant eye of the Indian noticed that in the very center of the circle was a little worm, crawling across the dry leaves. When he had drawn the circle, the man of God reached over, took a flaming brand from the fire, and touched it to the leaves, here and there, till there blazed a complete circle of leaping flames. As the fire burned among the leaves, it came closer and closer to the center of the circle, cutting off all means of escape from the little worm. The flames burned closer and closer to the worm—the tiny creature squirmed, sought a way of escape, but found none. And as the fire closed in and dried up the moisture from its wriggling body, it cringed and curled up to die.

Then the man reached down his hand into the burning flames and touched the ground in the center of the circle, right at the spot where the little creature lay. The worm crawled up on the man's hand, lifted it up and held it safely away from the fire.

During all this time the Indian watched carefully. His keen eye missed no detail. Then the missionary raised his eyes to the chief and spoke the softly, "I was just like that worm—helpless and lost. I deserved to be destroyed because I had been God's enemy. Because of all the badness in me, the fire of the condemnation of the wrath of God was closing in around me. There was no escape. I was powerless to save myself. I had no hope."

"But then God's strong Son—whose name is Jesus—came to the earth and let them nail Him to die on a great cross. You see, He suffered for my punishment. He bore the flames of God's wrath in my place. He reached down to where I was to save me out of the fire."

"He came to the world that He had made," continued the missionary, "and the world turned its back on Him. He came to his own people, and they didn't receive Him. They turned Him away. But in all the earth those who said 'Yes' to Him, received Him. To all of them the strong Son of God gave power to become His own and to turn from bad to good—from death to life—if they were willing to look up and trust Him—like this little worm trusted me to save it from the flames."

Where once the leaping flames danced brightly, now only glowing embers remained, and the moon, which had hovered over the horizon when first the two men met, now rode high in the sky. They knelt together beside the fire.

The Indian raised his hands and heart to Heaven and cried out, "Oh, Great Spirit God, oh, strong Jesus God, reach down here, save bad Indian from fire, make bad Indian good Indian by Your strong power."

The Indian leaped to his feet—his face shining in triumph. He stood for a moment, gazing into the star-studded sky, then turned and disappeared in silence midst the trees of the forest.

CAMPFIRE

The man of God knelt beside the fire saying, "Oh, everlasting Father, speak to this man's heart, show him how to grow, to obey Thee, to fulfill Thy will for his life."

"He was dressed in all the full regalia of his position in the tribe. The great war bonnet of eagle feathers crowned his brow, falling on both sides almost to the ground."

CAMPFIRE

ENOUGH

Fall turned to winter. Snows came. A great white blanket covered the surface of the ground in that far northern woodland. During the long winter evenings, the man of God spent much time praying for the Indian Chieftain who had come to Christ. During those same long winter evenings, the Indian was spending much time preparing for that which he would bring as a gift to his Savior and God.

When the snows began to thaw, the green shoots came out upon the trees, and the first early spring flowers began to rise among the dead leaves of the previous autumn. Again, as the evening call echoed across the lake, and as the man of God waited beside his fire, the chieftain appeared between the parting boughs of the young firs that circled the spot where the flames of the campfire glowed and flickered.

In his hands the man brought an object that was beautiful to behold—a trinket made of silver and turquoise. It was the fruit of the most skilled handcraft of the men of the forest. He presented it to the missionary with these words,

"I bring a gift for my God."

The missionary looked into the Indian's eyes and answered just two words, "Not enough."

Without another word the chieftain disappeared among the trees of the forest.

Springtime came in full bloom. Blossoms came out on the trees. Flowers broke through the ground and blossomed in their full glory. When the beginnings of the summer had arrived, the Indian chief at the hour of sunset came again to the campfire spot of the man of God. This time in his hands he brought something which was not a useless trinket, but rather an instrument essential to his life—his constant companion both on the warpath and on the hunt—his arrows and his bow.

Holding them out before the missionary, he said, "I bring a better gift for my Savior, for my God."

Knowing that this indeed was something so necessary to his life, that it meant a real sacrifice, the missionary looked into the eyes of the chief and answered just two words, "Not enough."

The Indian turned and disappeared among the trees of the forest, and the man of God prayed.

Summer came to its full verdure, and then the harvest time, when all the fruits of the land were gathered in. In the peak of the harvest time, at the hour of the eventide when the Indian evening call was echoed across the lake, again the Indian approached the man of God. This time he held in his hand the thing that was indeed the most precious possession of any Indian warrior, his blanket. Skillfully woven by the most skilled artisans of his tribe, it bore in its very design the history of all his exploits and deed of bravery, which led to his having become the chief of the tribe. He brought it in his hands and holding it up and with pride in his voice, he spoke these words,

"I bring my best gift for my Savior and my God."

The missionary knew enough of the culture of the Indian tribes to appreciate indeed the value of the great sacrifice the man was making. Understanding all of this and looking into the eyes of the man who came before him, he answered just two words, "Not enough."

Again, without speaking further the chief disappeared among the trees of the forest. The man of God prayed.

Autumn's season wore on. The leaves on the trees again turned to their riot of brilliant color, then faded, then fell from the trees, spreading their carpet of golden brown upon the surface of the woodland, and leaving the trees stretching long, dark fingers into the autumn sky.

As the first chill of winter came, the man of God sat beside the fire, huddling close to appreciate the warmth of the flames. He listened as the Indian evening call echoed in the distance.

"Ya-a-a-ah Ha-a-ah we-e-e-e hay-y o-o-oh."

CAMPFIRE

As the last sound died out and as the last long rays of crimson disappeared in the west, the boughs of the fir trees were parted, and into the circle stepped the Indian chief.

He was dressed in all the full regalia of his position in the tribe. The great war bonnet of eagle feathers crowned his brow, falling on both sides almost to the ground. On his breast hung the sacred wampum of the tribe. There were bracelets on his arms and ankles, and from his shoulders hung the beautiful blanket depicting the history of his exploits as chieftain of the tribe.

In his hands he brought nothing.

Without a word, he approached the fire. Raising his hands, he lifted the great war bonnet from his head and dropped it into the flames and watched as the fire consumed the trophy. Then the sacred wampum from his breast followed into the fire. From his arms and ankles, he removed the jeweled bracelets and dropped them into the burning flames. From his shoulders, he removed the blanket, with the insignia of his rank and position in the tribe and gave it also to the flames.

Standing then as any Indian, dressed only in his loincloth, his hands empty, he fell to his knees and looking into the eyes of the man of God said, "I have nothing else. I bring my self—a gift for his Savior and my God." The missionary, standing in front of the Indian chief, looked into his eyes and said just one word, "Enough."

"There in the mountains was a spring-fed lake, crystal clear and blue as the sky. From this lake there was an abundant supply of water, and all the needs of the people, their cattle, gardens, and farms were met."

CAMPFIRE

CITY WITHOUT WATER

The story is told of a beautiful city that flourished in the middle of a vast, dry desert. Stretched out in all directions were the dry, desert sands. Still, the city was green and fertile, where exquisite flowers bloomed and sent their delightful perfume into the air. On the farms in this area the finest of corn and the best of vegetables grew. The city was a green emerald in the golden parched sand.

The secret to the city's life was a long, stout pipeline that stretched from afar to the city, bringing the water supply from a distant reservoir located high in the mountains. There in the mountains was a spring-fed lake, crystal clear and blue as the sky. From this lake there was an abundant supply of water, and all the needs of the people, their cattle, gardens, and farms were met. The people were so accustomed to the water supply, they didn't often think of where it came from or worry whether it would be always there.

But then the day came when one man noticed that the water was not as abundant as it used to be. It didn't seem to be coming as plentifully, and it began to drop off sharply on the same day. There was much less water than there had been before. The day following, the pipeline ceased to pour forth the life-giving water. The supply had stopped.

In a panic the people began to seek water. Some brought it in barrels from a distant city, but they soon realized that they could not continue to exist. One after another they abandoned their homes, went in wagons, and whatever way they could travel to other cities where there was an abundant supply of water, where the rivers and lakes were to be found. In a matter of a very few days, the city became an abandoned ghost town— hardly anyone had stayed. Life was impossible then.

And so, the days and weeks went by, stretching into months. Then it just so happened that two young men who had lived in that city went for a hunting trip high up in the very mountains where the reservoir was located.

One of them said to the other, "Let us climb to the high place where the reservoir was, where the clear blue water used to be, and let us find out why the water no longer lies full and abundant in that lake."

So the two young men, being strong of heart and sturdy of limb, made the climb. When they reached the high place in the mountains where they expected to see the high basin of the reservoir, they were amazed to find—not a dry valley as they had expected—but a large, clear, blue lake, overflowing with more than enough water.

"What can be the reason?" asked one of the other. They explored and found that the pipeline was still there, but it was dry. Upon careful examination, they found that a plug had been placed in the pipeline that completely stopped the water flow from the still abundant lake. Carefully and with much effort, they withdrew the piece of wood. When they had done this, the water flowed forth with great force, washing out the accumulated rust and dirt.

Shortly afterward, they returned to their city to find that the water supply was just as abundant and strong as ever before. The word spread, and all those who had lived in the city previously returned and rejoiced in the abundance. But they only regretted the fact that they need not have suffered the lack of water, they need not have suffered the loss, if they had only known to pull the plug.

CAMPFIRE

A SLAVE SET FREE

Zondu was an African boy who lived in a little village in the interior of the dark continent. Never in his life had he seen the terrible things he saw that day—which turned out to be the most fateful day in his life and in the village's life. Men with white faces came stalking through the woods, each carrying a stick—a magic stick that barked terrible noise and fire at one end.

Zondu could remember his father—strong and brave, standing at the door of the hut. And as he stood protecting his family, suddenly one of the sticks barked out, and Zondu's father fell dead. After that it was hard for him to remember just what happened. There was a long, tiresome trek through the forest then they finally came to the shore of the sea.

Zondu remembered being herded together with other captives into the hold of a great ugly ship that rode deep in the sea. He could remember the tossing and rolling of the ship as it plowed through the ocean waves—day and night, day and night. It was hard to distinguish the days from the nights because so little light came through the deck into the hold below, where he and his fellow tribesmen were chained. His mother became very sick. Days later she was carried out. Zondu never saw her again.

After many days the boy heard the sound of the rubbing of the ship against the dock. At last he saw the clear light of day. Zondu had come to America to be sold as a slave.

A SLAVE SET FREE

He remembered that great auction block where he was sold, then carried away to a cotton plantation. There, as a boy, he knew nothing but hard work and ill-treatment. Day after day he worked in the cotton fields. He grew taller and became very strong. He was the strongest of all the young slaves of the plantation. When he reached the age of nineteen, he was taken back—back again to the city where once again he mounted the auction block. Here again he was sold. This time he was worth a much greater price. The auctioneer sold all the other slaves first, then paused as Zondu stood alone on the auction block—a strong man and valuable slave.

"Who will bid five hundred dollars for this excellent slave?" called the auctioneer to the great crowd.

Someone said, "Five hundred dollars" another, "Five hundred and fifty" another, "Six hundred" another, "Seven hundred."

Zondu looked out across the great crowd. Out on the fringe of the crowd stood a tall man apart from the rest, looking at the whole spectacle with disdain. He stood beside a great coach drawn by four shining black horses.

Another man countered, "Eight hundred and fifty dollars."

"Nine hundred dollars," "Nine hundred and fifty dollars."

The man with the black horses called out, "One thousand dollars." Everyone stood amazed. It was the highest price paid for a slave for many years.

The auctioneer took Zondu with a chain on his wrist through the crowds to the tall man at the edge of the crowd, and hauling him over to him, together with the key, said, "Yours for a thousand dollars."

He received the sum and went back toward the block. The owner of the coach turned the key in the lock which held the chain to Zondu's wrist and let the chains fall. Zondu was about to reach down to pick up the chains.

"No," said the other, "we'll not need them. Come with me."

Walking over to the coach, Zondu saw the man take a satchel from the coach from which he drew a quill, a horn of ink, and a paper.

"What is your name?"

"My name is Zondu," replied the slave.

Writing for a moment, and blotting it, the man turned the paper over to the young man and said, "This is your freedom paper. You are no longer a slave. You are free."

"Free!" The wonder of the word was so great that he could hardly understand it.

CAMPFIRE

Zondu stood paralyzed with amazement. He stared at the paper, barely realizing what it was. He grasped it to him, then without so much as speaking a single word to him who had freed him, he turned and ran—ran as fast as he could—ran away from the horrible auction block—ran away from the city—ran away from those great wharves where the ships plied their trade from Africa. He ran as fast as he could, away from all that spoke of slavery and bondage.

"Free," he shouted aloud, leaping and dancing with joy. Anyone seeing him certainly would have thought he was crazy, but Zondu was so happy with his freedom that he didn't care what anyone thought. The afternoon wore on, and at last the sun reached the horizon and disappeared behind it. Long rays of light stretched across the sky, painting it with all the soft and beautiful colors of the sunset. As the shadows lengthened across the cotton fields, and the lights came on in the little cottages, Zondu began to listen to the strumming of the banjos and the singing of the spirituals by the slaves in their cabins.

Suddenly there entered into his mind for the first-time thoughts that had not come before. "Where was he going? What was he going to do? Where would he find a bed tonight? Where would he have supper? Where could he join in the fellowship of others, strumming the banjo, listening to familiar songs?"

He looked about him and knew that he was alone. Nowhere in the world was anyone that cared for him. No longer did he leap for joy. No longer was he running. He lifted one tired foot after the other in plodding weariness.

Hardly realizing what he was doing, Zondu stopped in his tracks, turned slowly around, and began to walk back in the direction from which he had come, still clutching the paper in his hand. Then his pace began to quicken a little. He began to run. Back toward the city he sped, back toward the auction block, back toward the great wharves from which he had run with such joy earlier that afternoon. He was running like a man possessed.

It was late that night when Zondu again reached the city. A question here and a question there, and he started out again from the city, out along the highway toward the west. As he ran, he questioned all he saw. In the early hours of the morning, Zondu reached a highway inn. There he saw the coach beside the inn. Beyond, he could hear the munching of the black horses in the stalls. Running quickly to the door of the inn, he knocked again and again. At last the keeper of the inn opened the door a crack and looked out. On seeing a black man there, he slammed the door again, but Zondu was insistent.

"Let me come in! Let me come in! I must see the man who owns these horses and coach!"

The innkeeper refused to open.

A SLAVE SET FREE

Suddenly, a kindly voice came from the upstairs room, "Friend, let the man come up. I am waiting for him."

Reluctantly the innkeeper opened the door.

Zondu climbed the stairs and entered the room where the owner of the coach and horses sat waiting for him. Falling down on his knees before him, he threw the paper at his feet and cried, "Sir, I don't want to be free. Take this paper back. I want to be your slave."

Then, looking into his eyes, the man said kindly, "No, Zondu, you can't be my slave, for I have no slaves, but you can serve me. I need you to work on my plantation, not as a slave, but as a free man. I will pay you wages."

Then the joy that Zondu felt was greater than any he had known before. He had come back to the one in all the world who cared for him. Willing to be a slave, but now, not as a slave but as a free man, he served his master and received his reward. He had the greatest joy that he could know.

CAMPFIRE

THE MOUNTAIN STREAM

Tom and Bill were brothers, twin brothers. They looked so much alike that no one who did not know them very well could tell the difference. But Tom and Bill could tell the difference. They loved to do all kinds of exciting things like every boy does—they especially liked to hike. As little boys, they had always looked forward to the day when they would be big enough to hike to the top of the mountain that was not far from the village. From the top of that mountain, one could see hundreds of miles in every direction.

And then one day when they were about your age, Tom and Bill decided they were ready to make the trip. They laid their plans carefully, prepared a lunch to carry along, got up early one morning, long before daybreak, and began their hike. When the first rays of sunlight came over the horizon, they had already started their ascent. Up and up they went with enthusiasm. When they passed the timberline, it was still midmorning. They could look off in the distance where they could see villages and towns, rivers and valleys that they had never seen before. But up they went, past the level of the low clouds. They could look down and see the fleecy, white clouds huddled like a flock of sheep below them. The boys would stop and rest every once in a while and talk about the view that they could see.

At last they reached the pinnacle. How amazing it was to look in all directions between the billowing clouds and see mountains, valleys, rivers, villages, towns and cities!

THE MOUNTAIN STREAM

After a little while of gazing at the breath-taking scenery, they started down, but instead of going back the same route by which they had climbed, they took another trail. Soon after they started down from the summit of the mountain, they came to a beautiful little spring, sparkling out of a small cave on the mountainside, sending water down in a little trickling stream.

"This would be a great place to have our lunch," Tom suggested.

"Okay," replied Bill, "let's stop right here."

So, they stopped in the shade of the rocks beside the spring, opened their lunch, enjoyed the moments of rest, and drank the clear cool water. Then as they started down Bill said to Tom, "I think I'll cross the stream and go down on the other side because that's the side we live on, you know."

"I think I'll stay on this side," replied Tom. "I want to find out what it's like over here."

Without thinking much more about it, Bill stepped across the bubbling rivulet and started down on the other side of the stream. Tom continued on his side. They walked along with the little stream between them. Other springs fed their waters into the stream, and it grew wider and deeper. It became a brook. As they walked, they had to talk louder to hear each other.

"Hey," called Bill to Tom, "when are you going to come across?"

"Oh, that's easy," called his brother, "look, I could just hop right across on these stones." "Okay, come on," replied Bill.

"Aw, no, I think I'll stay on this side a while longer."

So, they went on down, and the brook became deeper and wider, as other brooks and streams poured their water into it. The crossing would evidently be more difficult the further they went.

"Say, Tom," called Bill at the top of his voice sometime later, "how are you going to get across? Remember, we live on this side."

"Sure, I know, look, it will be easy, I can just climb that big tree that's hanging right across the brook."

"Yeah, that's right," Bill noticed. "Come on then, this is a good chance."

"Aw, no," Tom replied, "I'd rather stay on this side and see what it's like. You go ahead. I'll go down this side. I can always swim across." And so, they went on down the mountainside.

The brook became a creek and then a river. The deep current was swift because the water came from high in the mountain. Hardly realizing it, the boys were coming closer and closer to the mouth of the river. They could hear in the distance the rumbling roar of the river's mighty current. They were shouting back and forth, as loud as they possibly could, using gestures to make their meaning clearer.

How was Tom going to get across? Finally, not having the ambition to go back upstream to where the tree had stretched across, he decided to try to swim across. He dove into the river and tried to swim against the swift current. Even though he was a strong swimmer, his strokes seemed to get him nowhere. Caught in the middle of the stream, he was carried by the current right out into the big river.

Poor Bill, standing helpless on the bank did not know what to do. He saw his brother washed out into the middle of the river, and then he realized with a shock that it would not be long before the more powerful current of the larger river would carry him right to the brink of a great waterfall, where he would be dashed to pieces.

He cried out in alarm, but then realized that no one could possibly hear his voice. The spot was a long way from the nearest road or house, and the din of the rushing water and the thunderous waterfall drowned out his voice completely.

Racing along the bank, watching his helpless brother, Bill noticed suddenly that a whirlpool seemed to catch Tom in the current of the large river. It carried him around and brought him for a moment closer to the shore. Leaping onto an outstretched limb of a tree, Bill tossed the end of his shirt to his brother. Tom grabbed it, and Bill was just barely able to haul him to safety. Pulling him out on the shore, Bill found that Tom was utterly exhausted, barely able to stand. He rubbed him dry and massaged his muscles. Tom at last was able to struggle to his feet. With Bill half-carrying Tom, the two boys reached home late that night. Bill had walked the same distance that day, but he had walked all day on the side of the stream that was toward their house—what a difference! Tom had almost lost his life.

"At first, he struggled, but looking into the eyes of the wounded one, he stood tall and carried the cross, heavy though it was."

CAMPFIRE

THE MAN ON THE CROSS

Two sturdy boys trudged up a long, winding road that led from the seaport of Joppa toward the great city of Jerusalem. They were tired. The journey had been long and arduous. But, despite their weariness, they were excited. This was the first time the two brothers had been permitted to accompany their father on his annual trip to the Holy City. Their father walked some distance ahead in the company of older men, while others followed behind. They were part of a great company going up to the city for their annual pilgrimage.

"Oh, Rufus," said the younger brother, "what a thrill to be going at last to the city of Jerusalem! I've imagined so many times what it must be like. I wonder if it will really be what we have always thought?"

Speaking with the superior wisdom of a year's seniority, the older brother said, "No doubt there will be many things that will be surprising to us. Yet I think I know what the temple will be like because we have read in the Holy Scriptures exactly what the specifications for it are. Even then I think there will be splendor beyond our imagination."

The boys were dreaming as they walked and talked. Sometime later, as they at last came in sight of the great city, they were walking closer to their father and noticed that a great multitude of people was emerging from one of the gates of the city. The crowd was shouting with a fervor. It seemed that they were bent on some hasty mission, some matter of great importance.

THE MAN ON THE CROSS

The boys began to speculate concerning the significance of what they saw. The crowd, having come out of the gate of the city, was making its way out to a little knob-shaped hill some distance from the city. As they came closer, the two boys noticed that in the center of the crowd, a man was walking very slowly, His shoulders bent under a load which seemed extremely heavy. The load was a great wooden beam to which was fastened a cross-beam.

"Oh, yes, Alexander," the older boy said, "this is how the Romans punish their criminals. Surely that man has done some terrible deed and is going out of the city with the soldiers."

"What will they do to him?"

"They are going to crucify him."

"How do they do that?"

"They lay the cross down and nail him to it, I think, or perhaps tie him to it with throngs. Perhaps we'll have a chance to see."

"But look at that man, Rufus. He certainly doesn't look like a criminal. Can you see his face?"

The boys were close enough now to see the face of the man. Simon, their father, tall strong, and broad-shouldered had also seen the man who bore the cross. In fact, he had seen his face and was so impressed with what he had seen there, that Simon stood still in the road. Those he had been conversing with had gone on ahead in their excitement to reach the city of Jerusalem. But Simon had forgotten all about his mission for the moment because the look he had seen on the face of the man who bore the heavy cross was something that he could not explain, and it reached into his very heart.

The boys came closer to where their father stood. They stopped too.

"No, Alex, he doesn't look like a criminal. The soldiers are taking him, but it seems to me that he looks like the conqueror and that they are the captives."

As they looked, the boys noticed that the man who bore the heavy beam stumbled in the road and fell. As he did so, they saw blood gush from wounds on his back. They saw the weight of the heavy beams bear down upon him. With great effort he struggled and stood, taking one labored step then another. The older boy looked with admiration at the man.

"There's a strong man," he said.

But as he spoke, the man fell again then struggled to his feet once more, staggering on up the incline. In this way he came to the place where the man and his two sons stood watching, amazed at the spectacle which met their eyes. One

CAMPFIRE

of the soldiers, seeing strong

Simon standing in the way, seized him by the arm and said, "We'll never get there this way. Here's a strong man, let him take the cross." Simon hardly realized what was happening. Another soldier grabbed him by the other arm, and another pushed him from behind. He was projected into the center of the swarming crowd. They took the heavy cross-beam from the shoulders of the bleeding Man. Simon was not altogether unwilling to take the burden, because he was glad to see the other relieved, and yet he had no choice—he was compelled by the soldiers. At first, he struggled, but looking into the eyes of the wounded one, he stood tall and carried the cross, heavy though it was. The boys were lost in the multitude, but they tried to stay close to their father in the crowd and be near the man whose gaze had so impressed them.

They reached the top of the little knoll. There they saw that someone had dug a hole deep in the ground. On each side of this hole two crosses stood erect, each bearing its prisoner. Looking into the hard faces of those who hung in agony on the two crosses, the two boys realized that these two were criminals indeed.

"That's the kind of man you expect to see crucified," said Rufus, "but what about this one?"

The one they referred to was firmly gripped by the soldiers, his garments torn from him and then, when the cross that this man and Simon had carried up the hill was laid down, the bleeding man was stretched out. A great burly soldier took a heavy mallet and drove rude nails which tore into the flesh of the wounded one's hands and feet, nailing Him to the cross.

As the two boys watched, it seemed to them that each blow of the mighty mallet caused a shiver of pain to go through their own bodies. They watched the face of the man who was being so ill-treated. They did not see what they expected. Instead of a wince of pain, although it was evident that he was feeling great pain, there was a look of great, deep sorrow, as if He were more concerned for those who nailed Him to the cross than for himself. That's what the two boys came to believe as they watched.

Then when the cruel nailing was finished, all the soldiers together lifted up the great cross with its burden, putting the foot of the upright beam into the top of the hole that was dig. Then they let it fall. With one great thud the cross stood erect. They watched as the body sagged, and all the joints were pulled out. He hung there, a shapeless form. Even then his face was that of a conqueror. The man's eyes met the eyes of the boys and their father. The eyes of a victor, not of one who was vanquished.

The events which followed greatly impressed them all, things they would never forget—how the very sky seemed to go into mourning. They heard the captain of the soldiers cry out, "This, indeed, was the Son of God!"

The boys talked for many days afterward. They wondered, "Who could he have been? He was, indeed, no ordinary man. Who could he have been? Who was the man on the cross? Who was he?

When Simon and his two sons went into the city of Jerusalem that evening, the questions concerning the man on the cross were the subject of all their conversation and thought.

They knew they would not forget what they had seen that afternoon. In ensuing weeks, the two boys often thought of the events of that day, even though their time was filled with the exciting adventure of exploring the city of Jerusalem and seeing with their own eyes the things of which they had read throughout the years of their young lives.

Simon, their father, had often visited Jerusalem before from his home in faraway Cyrene. Still, this visit was different for him too from any other. As he went about the routine of his religious observances, his mind never wandered far from the man on the cross. He heard men talking of Him in many of the small places that dotted the city of Jerusalem. Simon learned that there was a group of simple country Galileans who had banded together in the name of the man on the cross. They believed that this one was the very Messiah who was to come to save the people from their sin. Could it be true?

He sought every opportunity to talk to these Galileans, and frequently in the early evening when he and his two boys would sit together discussing the events of the day, Simon would bring them news of his conversations with the men who believed in the man on the cross.

"But Father," asked the older boy, " how could it be that he is the Messiah, when he died, and he died the death of a slave?"

"Well, my son, the Galileans teach that although he died, He also arose on the third day, and walked upon the Earth again, and then ascended into Heaven."

As he talked of these events, he marveled at the way these things fit with the Scriptures, and the prophecy which said his hands and feet would be pierced, with the prophecy which said the chosen one would be a man of sorrows and acquainted with grief, and with the prophecy stating that he would suffer, and by suffering, he would save his people.

Days went by and Simon grew to take more and more interest in learning from these Galileans about those things which concerned the Man who had died on the cross. Sometimes Rufus and Alexander, the boys, would go with him to that great

CAMPFIRE

barely finished upper room where these men gathered.

Then the day came when as they were all gathered together in the upper room, praying and speaking of the things of this man whom they called Christ, suddenly something happened that was very difficult to describe or explain. There was a great sound as of a voice, and yet it didn't seem like a voice but more like the sound of a mighty, rushing wind. All of these men waited expectantly for some manifestation of the power of God. They realized that this indeed must be the comforter, the Holy Spirit, would come and give strength.

The boys, sitting in the corner, saw that their father was deeply moved and all the other men with him. These men, who had been speaking of the things of Christ heretofore only in secret in whispered conversation, now seemed mightily changed.

One of them, a rough fisherman called Peter, stood up and spoke. As he talked, it seemed as if his voice had the power of fire, and he began to tell them clearly and in a way that was very plain just what the truth was concerning this man who was called the Christ.

"Listen to him talk!" said Alexander to his older brother. "He's talking our language!"

"Yes, it's extraordinary," replied the older boy. "Look over there. Those men are from Arabia, and they don't know our language or the language of the Jews, but they seem to understand this man too!" Then, as the boys watched, it was clear that by some great miracle power of God, every man and boy in that whole large room heard Peter talking as if he were talking to each of them in his own language.

As soon as the wonder of this miracle was over, the boys focused their eyes on Peter and listened closely to the words that he was speaking. Peter talked of Jesus, the Son of God. He told them how He had been crucified and had been slain. The boys remember well the very sight that they had seen. Then Peter told them that, according to the prophecy of the Old Testament, the crucified one did not stay in the grave, and appeared to one and another of those who believed in him. Then he ascended into Heaven, leaving the promise that the Holy Spirit would come in power.

As Peter spoke, all the people who heard him felt as if a great piercing sword of truth had struck to their very hearts—and it was the sword of truth of the Word of God.

Then it was that the man Peter said, "Repent and be baptized every one of you for the remission of sin, and ye shall receive the gift of the Holy Ghost."

In the days following, the boys accompanied their father to their own town.

THE MAN ON THE CROSS

They went with hearts full of joy because they had come to know Christ and the power of his Holy Spirit, and now they were going back to their own people to make him known.

CAMPFIRE

WHERE IS THE CHRISTIAN?

In the ancient city of Rome, a young lad named Gaius was walking along the street with his buddy Marcellus talking about the strange things that were happening in the city of Rome in those days—about how those followers of that strange sect from Palestine believed that one called Jesus, who had died, had risen again and was alive. They were spreading the word of their belief among many people in Rome, and the emperor had forbidden all that believe in such things. No Roman could have any king except Caesar himself.

They talked about the guards who would go about hailing citizens on the street, saying, "Lord Caesar," calling Caesar Lord and God.

Those who were not Christians would answer "Lord Caesar," but those who had come to believe in Jesus Christ would only answer, "Lord Christ," because they had no other Lord. Caesar was their king. But only Christ Jesus was their Lord.

The boys had seen how Christians were cast to the lions and were torn to pieces, others were cut in pieces by the sword, still others were tied to posts, their garments soaked in oil, and burned to death.

"Why is it," asked Gaius, "that when there is such terrible persecution there are still those who believe in this Jesus? I think they are crazy."

"I don't think they are crazy," replied Marcellus. "I think they have something that the rest don't have."

WHERE IS THE CHRISTIAN?

"What do you mean, Marcellus?" Gaius asked quickly. It seemed as if Marcellus was defending them.

"I mean, Gaius, that I am a Christian."

"What? Don't you know they will kill you?" It didn't seem possible, but Marcellus was serious.

Marcellus stepped close to his friend and whispered, "Come to this spot tonight, when it is dark, and I'll show you what I mean."

That night, at the hour when all was dark, Gaius moved away from his house and found his way stealthily back to the place where he had left his friend that afternoon. The shadows were deep. He saw no one. "Ah," he thought with some relief, "Marcellus has forgotten, I will go home." At that moment, he felt a hand on his shoulder. He whirled around in panic only to find his buddy standing right behind him.

"Follow me," the older boy whispered, leading him away from the city out toward the outskirts of town. Gaius suddenly felt a chill of horror as he realized that Marcellus was leading him out in the cold black, darkness to the place of the tombs. He wanted to turn and run, but he was afraid to be alone. He followed. They walked among the very graves. They came to the mouth of a huge cave. Marcellus took hold of Gaius' arm and led him inside where, to his amazement, the frightened boy saw a rough, rock-hewn stairway, tunneling downward into the earth, lightened by a tiny, flickering torch concealed among jagged, shadowy rocks.

Marcellus took a light from the torch and went down the passageway into the very earth. They found a weird winding labyrinth of narrow caves underneath the surface of the earth. They were in the famous catacombs made by the pagans of that time, a place in which to bury their dead! The Romans believed that evil spirits would come to look for the dead but that they would get lost in the weird underground labyrinth. As Marcellus led him along, the younger boy wondered how he could find his way. "How do you know where you are going?"

"Look," Marcellus answered, holding the torch close to the cave. They could see the form of a little fish scratched into the side of the rock. The fish's head pointed in the direction in which they were going.

That fish was used as a sign, because the letters which begin the Greek words, "Jesus Christ, God's Son, Savior." These five words were the creed of those early Christians.

As the boys continued through the dark passage, they came suddenly to a large cave lighted by many torches. There they saw men, women and young people and

CAMPFIRE

heard them singing hymns of joy. An older man told them about the love of the Lord Jesus Christ.

That night before he went back to his house, Gaius fell to his knees and called out to the Lord Jesus Christ to come into his heart and save him from sin.

Gaius walked slowly along the Appian way. He was thinking about the wonder of his new salvation, about the amazing things he had learned about prayer, asking the Lord to give him strength to live and be faithful to Him. Suddenly, he heard a horrible din. Soldiers were running, clanking in their armor. In front of them ran a man, a Christian. Gaius knew that he had seen him that night in the torch-lit cavern. As the soldiers chased, the fugitive came near to where the boy stood. Then he disappeared into a passageway between two buildings.

The running soldiers came to the spot where Gaius stood. The captain brusquely asked him, "Where is the Christian?"

The question echoed in Gaius' heart. What should he say? The man they had been chasing was actually his brother in Christ. They were out to capture him, throw him to the lions or burn him to death, or perhaps cut him to pieces.

"Where is the Christian?" repeated the captain roughly.

What should he say? He knew what he would say. Gaius looked straight into the eyes of the captain as he answered:

"Sir, I am a Christian."

"The captain stood on top of the wooded hill, studying with much concern the face of the sky."

CAMPFIRE

EL CAPITAN

The captain stood on top of the wooded hill, studying with much concern the face of the sky. Before dawn he must make the attack—go through the pass to surprise the enemy troops. This was a maneuver requiring only about a dozen men. One by one he was thinking of the names of those men he was sure he could count on. His heart sank within him. Oh, if only he had those men who had once fought with him through these jungles, if only they could have been with him now for this greatest time of testing for his company! Sadly, he turned back, his gray head bowed, his face lined with concern. He returned slowly to the place where he had left the few untried soldiers who remained with him, cut off from supplies, and cut off from all contact with army headquarters.

All that remained were twelve inexperienced men, sufficient ammunition for the job, and each had his rifle—that was all. As he came close to the spot where the men had stopped to rest and build a campfire, he felt a premonition. Then he came closer and discovered that the worst of his fears were justified.

The men had deserted.

Something must have happened to scare them off because they had not even taken their arms. There were the rifles stacked. There was the ammunition. There were the smoldering ashes of the campfire. A look of disgust spread across his face. Soldiers? No, they were not soldiers—they were cowards. Now he was alone. There remained that last charge to be made. A surprise attack on the enemy

EL CAPITAN

stronghold could succeed and with just a few men. There would be reinforcements then, but everything depended on him, and now he was alone!

The captain looked out over the valley. There he could see the stalwart Indians trudging homeward through the evening twilight to their pueblo, a typical village of the Andes. These were stalwart, strong, silent men. He turned back, studied again the gray ashes and the wisp of smoke rising from what once had been a campfire.

The setting sun stretched long, crimson figures all across the sky and disappeared into the distant blue waters of the Pacific. Laborers from the dry, parched fields walked slowly home to the Indian village. There was a restlessness among the people—deep concern because there had been no rain. There was apprehension and fear among the people. Enemy forays were raiding villages in all that part of the country. But word of hope had come. It was rumored that El Capitan, a strong champion of the people, hovered near with a band of picked soldiers. He was the great hope and legend of the people. Robbers had molested one village for years until one dark night when El Capitan had appeared as from nowhere with a tiny band of men. From that night on the village had enjoyed peace and quiet.

Kidnappers had carried off the little daughter of the chief of another pueblo and had thrown all the people into consternation. Then one night El Capitan had ridden through the village at midnight and the child was back with her parents telling of an incoherent tale of incredible bravery on the part of her rescuers. The kidnappers had never returned.

A fierce mountain lion had long raided the flocks of another mountain village. El Capitan had passed through, and the great, tawny beast was found next morning—slain in the plaza of the village.

Such was the power and valor of El Capitan, but now his legendary form had not been seen for many days. The soldiers that marched with him, who so often had turned back the bandits, seemed to have lost their power.

Two old men were among those who left their fields that restless night at the hour of sunset and started back to the village. The walked more slowly and had farther to go than the rest and so were separated from the crowd. Suddenly they saw a masked form dressed in a dark robe, coming down from the mountain. He approached them.

"I come in peace," rumbled the dark-robed one.

"Who are you?" quavered the fear-stricken old men.

"It is El Capitan," came the deep-voiced reply. The two hurried toward him.

Night fell. The elders of the village sent the word around for all to meet in the

CAMPFIRE

plaza. The men and women of the village gathered. Suddenly a mysterious form appeared among them. He was dressed in a dark cloak, on his head the traditional witch doctor's headpiece with the horns of a bull. Speaking in a strange, sonorous tone, he addressed the people.

"Men of the village, today is a day of great danger. The enemy comes through the shadows, the drought is attacking our fields. The god of the village requires a sacrifice."

There was silence. Two more dark-robed figures appeared and stretched a great veil between two trees. Standing before the great veil, the tall one continued to speak. "From among the bravest of the men of his village, the god of the village calls for ten men to give themselves in sacrifice."

It was very dark. Only a glaring, winking oil lamp lit the group. Strained faces peered into the eyes of the tall one. Ten men must shed their blood to save the village. As he waited, fear froze the hearts of the people. There was perfect silence.

Silence. At last a young man stood. Trembling, pale, he stepped forward and stood beside the tall one.

The two disappeared behind the great veil—there was a sound of a knife against flesh. The people saw blood flow out from beneath the curtain.

The robed one returned, his knife blade bathed in crimson blood of the sacrifice.

"Who will be next? Nine more must die." A moment of silence. A father stood with one last lingering glance of affection at his wife and son, and then out of love for them, he strode forward, head held high, though trembling.

He too disappeared behind the veil with the tall one. The knife was drawn, blood flowed, the "priest" returned alone and stood staring out at the people.

An old man, grizzled with the work of many years, stood and moved behind the curtain, the stroke of the knife, the flow of blood.

Again, the robed figure appeared alone. "Come, strong ones," he shouted. A young lad stepped forward, barely the age to do the work of a village life and to suffer the hardships of manhood. Again, they disappeared, and the "priest" returned alone, his knife bathed in blood. And also, with the fifth, sixth, seventh, eighth, ninth, and tenth.

"And now," said the mysterious visitor, "the sacrifice is received. The village will be delivered." Again, he disappeared behind the curtain.

The people of the village waited—would he again appear?

A long time they waited, and then one of the men reached forward, took hold of the veil, pulled it aside fearfully, and stood in consternation. Another came and

EL CAPITAN

together they removed the veil. The people stared. The "priest" was gone. The ten who had gone forward to sacrifice themselves to save the village were nowhere to be seen. Instead, they saw only the slaughtered remains of ten sheep lying in their blood. Mystified and trembling with fear, the people of the village returned to their huts.

Late that night, as the moon rose over the mountain, the silent forms of eleven armed men crept silently over the pass.

The legendary El Capitan made the surprise attack on the enemy stronghold, united the liberation forces, and the scourge of the hills was defeated and put to route.

THE LUCKY STONE

Billy was just a little fellow. One day as he was walking along scuffing his feet, he happened to kick up a little stone. He watched the way it rolled, noticed that it seemed to have a little color to it, so he picked it up, juggled it in his hand a little while, and then popped it into his pocket. Somehow, he liked the feel of it and so kept it in his pocket day after day and called it his lucky stone.

Billy had a friend, an old craftsman, who worked as a lapidary in a jewelry store. His work was to polish precious stones and the forming of beautiful objects from gold, silver and other valuable metals. Billy loved to visit the lapidary and talk with him at the side of his bench. The old man enjoyed it too. Often, he would tell stories and talk to Billy of many interesting things. Sometimes he would even try to teach him some of his exceptional skills in the working of gold and silver.

One day as Billy sat talking with the old craftsman, he took the little stone out of his pocket to play with it. He'd become quite fond of it and had determined that he would keep it forever.

The craftsman suddenly looked at him and said, quite surprisingly, "Billy, give me that stone."

The boy quickly closed his fist and said, "Oh, that's nothing but a lucky stone I picked up."

"Give it to me, Billy."

THE LUCKY STONE

"Oh, it's just a little old stone," Billy pouted, then put it back in his pocket.

"Give me the stone, Billy."

The boy was embarrassed by the request, but he started talking about something else, and a few minutes later he left the shop. He felt rather funny about having refused the thing that the man had asked, but it was his idea that since it was a lucky stone, he must keep it himself, and never let anyone else have it.

For the next few days Billy did not go back to the jewelry shop because of his embarrassment. A week later, however, hoping that the whole incident had been forgotten, he went back to visit his friend again. As they talked, the man looked into Billy's eyes smiling, and said, "Son, give me your stone."

"What stone?"

"The stone in your pocket, Billy, give it to me."

"B-but."

"Give it to me, Billy," he insisted, "give me the stone."

Billy didn't lift his eyes to the old man's face but put his hand reluctantly into his pocket. Very slowly he extended his hand and dropped the stone into the upturned palm.

The man continued with his work, and a little later Billy left the shop still feeling uneasy and a little resentful that his friend had kept the stone.

Some days later when he came back into the shop, Billy was surprised to see that the craftsman had his stone on the table. With a chisel in one hand, and a small hammer in the other, he was hitting it, and turning it, and hitting it again, and again, and again, and again.

Curious, Billy sat down and watched. After a long time of having worked on the stone, suddenly a piece came off. Billy could see that inside was a brilliant green gem the color of clear, cool water. Day after day as the old man continued to work, Billy saw forming before his eyes, a beautiful and precious emerald. When it was finished, and polished, he held it for Billy to see. The sunlight shining on it caused iridescent rays to sparkle out.

It was a beautiful gem. As he reached out to take it, the man withdrew his hand. "No, Billy, one doesn't play with a stone like this." With great care he put it back into his strongbox, wrapping it in a piece of white velvet.

"But isn't it my stone?"

"Yes, Billy, it is your stone. Perhaps it will send you to college or build you a fine home someday. Perhaps it will do something even better than that, but one

CAMPFIRE

doesn't play with this kind of stone."

"But why didn't you tell me?" asked Billy.

Then the wise old man turned from his work and looked right into Billy's eye's, "Son, I also wanted you to understand how God works with you. Our heavenly Father calls to you and says, 'My son, give Me your heart.'"

"Lots of boys say, 'My life is my own to do with as I want. I can live the way I like to.' It's your life, yes, but God wants it. When He says, 'My son, give Me your heart,' He means, 'Give me your life—just turn your whole self over into My hand.' At first, many boys don't want to do that. They want to hold on to life and play with it. But one doesn't play with a stone like this, because it is precious.

"If you turn your heart and your life and everything into God's hand, He will work it, polish it in His way until it shines like a sparkling gem."

"That, son, is the storehouse that contains everything necessary for the completion of the garden."

CAMPFIRE

GOD'S GARDEN

A boy named Steve was walking along a familiar street in his home town when he noticed a high wall on the other side of the street. He'd seen the wall before but hadn't thought about what was behind it. Now he noticed that the gate in the center of the wall was open, and when he crossed the street and looked inside, he was amazed to find that it led to a garden so beautiful that it took his breath away.

There, before his eyes, shown a riot of gorgeous colors—harmonious rows of rare and exquisite flowers, blossoming bushes and shrubs, and trees heavily laden with colorful and delicious fruits. Neat paths wound their way in and out among the flowers and trees of the garden.

Steve stood in open-mouthed wonder, gazing at the marvelous beauty revealed through the open gate. How often had he passed by this gate before, without the slightest idea that anything so wonderful existed there!

His eye followed down the winding path, and he saw a suggestion of some building in the distance. Hardly realizing what he was doing, he took a step or two forward to see what was there in the center part of the garden. Grayish brown shingles showed through the boughs of the trees forming part of what seemed to be a log cabin nestled in between soft, green pines and hemlocks.

"Hello son!" Steve was suddenly startled by a man speaking softly. "Do you like my garden?"

GOD'S GARDEN

Whirling around, Steve looked toward the man. Why yes, sir!" gasped Steve, "It-it's the most beautiful garden I've ever seen in my life!"

"Then won't you please come right in?" replied the man with a little laugh. "I'm glad you like my garden, and I'd like to show it all to you."

Cautiously, Steve stepped forward and found himself in the midst of beauty such as he had never seen, even much more beautiful, in fact, than he had imagined as he stood in the street peering through the gate.

There were flowers and fruits such as he had never seen before, imported from foreign lands. He could see that everything was cared for by the skilled and loving hand of a Master-gardener—evidently the owner himself who was now showing him the garden.

Steve soon noticed one remarkable fact—the high wall enclosed a full acre of rich and fertile land, yet all the beauty that he had seen occupied only a tiny portion of the enclosed area. The great expanse of the enclosure lay clean and bare, ready to be cultivated.

He was puzzled by this and intended later to ask the man about it.

Steve came to the center of the garden where, in the midst the softly swaying evergreens, a grayish-brown log cabin came into full view. On closer observation Steve saw that there seemed to be two buildings—a very small house with a broad, shady, flagstone terrace stretching across the front of it, and beyond the house a large barn-like structure built right next to it.

As he walked around, Steve was surprised to see that the "barn" had no doors. It was built right on to the shingled cottage.

"How do you get into that?" Steve asked.

"Come around to the front of the house and I'll show you," returned the gardener.

The terrace, Steve discovered, was furnished with a large rocking chair and a long, low couch. A hammock swung between two posts. It seemed a most inviting place to rest. In the front of the house, approached from the terrace by two descending steps, there appeared a curious little door, so low that anyone would have to stoop down or kneel to go through it.

"The little door," explained the owner of the garden, "is the only entrance to this cottage and to the great storehouse."

"But what does the big storehouse have in it?" asked Steve, filled with curiosity.

"That, son, is the storehouse that contains everything necessary for the completion of the garden." Steve turned and saw the great expanse of rich uncultivated soil—the uncompleted part of the garden.

CAMPFIRE

Steve looked in wide-eyed wonder at all the beauties of the garden. He wanted to take it all in, for he didn't know whether he would have another chance to come into the enchanting garden.

The owner of the garden broke into Steve's reverie. "You like the garden, don't you son?"

"Sir, it's the most beautiful thing I've ever seen—I certainly do thank you for letting me come in to see it."

"I need a young man like you to care for the garden and to cultivate it until it is all complete—the whole garden—just as this part here by the gate." The gardener then turned very soft and gentle. "Would you like to do that?"

"I certainly would, sir!" was Steve's enthusiastic reply. His eyes fairly shown with joy at the wonderful prospect.

Steve walked through the garden and listened to the gardener explain about the work that needed to be done and how to do it. Then the owner of the garden told Steve the secret to the garden's beauty, "Today I leave the garden with you, son, care for it with all your heart and strength, but just inside that little low door is a telephone with a direct line to me. Every morning before you begin to work, and all during the day, whenever you need help, you call me up, and I will guide you as you search the storehouse for all the things you need."

With these words the gardener left, leaving Steve amid the flowers and fruit.

That afternoon, the excitement of exploring every little path and byway of the garden and of tasting each of the delicious fruits occupied Steve until sundown. As it began to get dark, he sat on the terrace, listening to the gentle evening sounds—crickets strumming miniature banjos, drowsy warblers settling minor arguments before going to bed, owls starting up exceptional hoots—and then Steve was asleep.

Bright dancing sunbeams shot through the pine boughs to waken Steve. He jumped up with a start, grabbing a shovel that he found on the terrace and hurrying out to begin his work in the garden. To his surprise and disappointment the soil that had appeared so soft and fertile seemed hard and difficult to work. He went to it with a will, however. After an hour or so, he had worked up a sweat, and yet he didn't seem to have made much progress. He kept trying, and it seemed to go much harder.

As the sun reached the top of its climb that day, and its fierce heat beat down on Steve's head, the boy stopped to mop his forehead and to view the results of his morning's work—a small bed of poorly turned soil.

"Hello there, fella!" Suddenly Steve heard a voice from somewhere near him.

GOD'S GARDEN

He looked around startled. At last he located the source of the voice—a man with a leather briefcase, sitting, of all places, on top of the garden wall! He appeared to be a salesman.

"You certainly are working hard, young man," said the salesman, as he climbed down inside the garden. "And it really isn't necessary you know."

He approached the boy and opened his briefcase. "Let me show you just the thing you need." He held up an envelope with a colored picture printed on it. "Here, my boy, you have a wholly new and wonderful type of seed. You don't need to do any hard work preparing the soil—just scatter the seed, and in three days you will see little green shoots. Very soon you will be eating of this beautiful and delicious fruit-"

"But, no sir," Steve finally managed to counter. "I don't need to buy any seed. Everything I need is here in the storehouse."

"Ha!" replied the salesman. "Once you've tried this seed, you'll not want any other kind. I'll tell you what. I'm going to give you a free sample. Just try it out." He thrust the envelope into Steve's hand.

The boy began to protest again but became intrigued by the picture on the envelope, as it showed a luxuriant vine with curious fruit of varying brilliant colors. Then he looked up to give it back to the salesman, but the salesman had disappeared!

Curious to know how this free sample seed would grow, Steve went back to the furthest corner of the enclosure, trying to ignore the uneasy feeling in his heart, and quickly opened the envelope, pouring the contents out on the ground. The seed was as fine as powder, and as he poured it out, the breeze caught it and spread it around a larger area than he had planned. He stood for a moment looking at the seed, then turned and walked slowly back to the terrace. There he stretched out on the couch.

The next day began much the same—but the work went even harder, and at the end of each day it seemed to Steve that he had less to show for his labor.

Each day, also, he found himself irresistibly drawn to the back corner of the garden. He was amazed at how soon the tiny green shoots appeared, where the seed had been sown and blown. In a few weeks' time there was a green tangled vine spreading all over the surface of the ground, climbing the walls and even reaching out toward the flowers and fruit trees in the beautiful part of the garden.

Then one day he noticed tiny, round, red and yellow berries. Eagerly he seized a handful and popped them into his mouth.

"Ugh!"—A look of consternation crossed Steve's face, and he quickly spit out the fruit. The fruit was bitter with a bitterness different from anything he had ever tasted. When he had spit out the fruit, there remained a strangely sweet aftertaste. Steve was intrigued, and somehow despite the bitterness, he couldn't resist the urge to taste it again. This time he slipped a tiny yellow berry between his lips. The berry tasted exotically sweet—different from anything he had ever tasted. Another berry followed, then another.

As he walked back toward the beautifully planted garden, Steve saw a great pear tree laden with ripe, luscious fruit. He picked a pear and began to eat it, but was astonished that it seemed insipid and tasteless to him. He tried apples, plums, and grapes, but none seemed to have any taste.

Frantically he rushed from tree to tree, tasting all the fruit of the garden. All were tasteless. Retiring to the terrace, Steve felt a heavy sadness come over him. Something had taken away all the pleasure he derived from the good fruit of the garden.

The next day and each succeeding day Steve would find himself running first to the back corner of the garden, watching the amazing growth of the strange vine he had planted and eating the bitter fruit—that seemed to taste sweeter each day.

He hardly noticed that day by day the beautiful fragrant flowers and blossoming shrubs were fading from neglect. Daily the vine grew until it overran first a part, then bit by bit, the whole garden. It blocked the gate and even closed in around the pines and hemlocks that circled the log cottage.

The day came, however, when Steve woke up to the fact that the delightful beauty of the garden was faded. The great rampant weed had invaded the flowered cloisters of fragrance and had choked the delicate color and perfume that had so spellbound Steve the day he had first found the garden.

He remembered with remorse the owner's words, "Today I leave the garden with you, son—care for it with all your heart and strength."

Steve was heartbroken. How miserably he had failed! What could he do? Then suddenly he remembered with a shock that he had forgotten completely the rest of the owner's counsel, "Just inside the little door is a telephone—"

The telephone!—And the storehouse! How could he have forgotten? He looked frantically for the little door, but it was entirely covered by the leaves of the rampant weed. However, he had an idea of the general location of it, and he hurried toward it.

Suddenly he heard a voice behind him, "Hey there, young fella, where are you going in such a hurry?"

He turned to see the grinning face of the salesman. "Why, I'm going to get help to get rid of this terrible, ugly vine that's ruining the garden," explained Steve, almost sobbing.

"Terrible? Ugly?" queried the man in seeming wonderment. "But why do you say that? Hasn't it grown well? Don't you like the fruit?"

"Well, yes," Steve admitted. "It has grown amazingly, and I do—that is, I've come to like the fruit."

"Of course," rejoined the salesman, "and you must agree that this green foliage is beautiful to behold."

As Steve talked with this man, his fears of the morning seemed to melt, and the vine's foliage seemed less ugly, just as the fruit had become less bitter. So it was that the great rampart weed continued to destroy the once beautiful garden.

Another day came when in the clear light of the early morning, Steve saw the garden as it was—a shambles, ruined by his disobedience to the owner.

Again he looked for the tiny door that led to help. He caught sight of the door and was hurrying toward it when again he heard the now familiar voice of the seed salesman.

This time, however, Steve kept hurrying toward the little door and refused to turn and look at the salesman. The door was so low that even by stooping down he could not enter. He had to fall on his knees and lower his head. Then he could go through the door.

As Steve lifted the telephone receiver, a tender voice answered immediately, "Hello, son, you need help, don't you?"

"Oh, yes, sir!" cried Steve, in heartbroken agony, "I have failed you miserably! I have neglected this wonderful garden and let it fade—I have planted strange seed—the garden is ruined!" Somehow Steve felt an indescribable peace when he had unburdened his heart.

"What do you want me to do?" the gardener came back over the wire.

"Oh, sir, help me! Save me from the terrible damage I've done to this garden." Somehow Steve felt sure that the owner of the garden could solve his problems completely.

"There is only one way, son," came the kind gardener again, "to get rid of the strange vine. There is only one person who can do it—my own Son."

"Oh, sir," cried Steve eagerly, "please, may he come to help me?"

The Son of the garden's owner—his only Son—met Steve at the little door. His Son, who looked into his heart with a look of love and said, "Steve, what can I do

CAMPFIRE

for you?"

"Please sir," answered Steve, "would you get rid of this weed. I can't do it. I don't know what to do to get rid of it."

"I can do it," said the owner's Son, "and I will if you want me to."

"Please sir, please do!"

Steve watched as the owner's Son went to the very place Steve had planted the seed. He reached down and grabbed the weed by the trunk—which was very large by now and had very sharp thorns—and He pulled it up by the roots and gathered it all together without regard to the sharp, hidden thorns that it bore, and threw it over the garden wall. As he came from the work, Steve saw that the thorns had wounded him severely in the hands and feet and in the head and in the side. As he saw the blood of this Man, the boy knew that it was flowing because he, Steve, had disobeyed.

The man who had cleared out the old weed spoke to him before He left him in the garden, "Never start a day without spending some time on the telephone and in the storehouse. That way my Father and I will always be with you."

The garden was empty and bare as Steve viewed it that day. His heart was sore as he realized how all the former beauty had been wasted, but he felt still more profound contentment when he thought of how the old weed was gone from the garden.

The next day, before he went to work, Steve went to the telephone—then into the storehouse. There he found refreshing food for his own strengthening, wonderful seed for planting in the garden, and tools for his work.

How different was the work that day! Steve thought he had accomplished more in that morning of work than in all the days put together since he had come into the garden. Throughout the afternoon and in the following days, Steve worked harder than he had ever worked in his life. He sang as he worked, and his joy knew no bounds.

Each morning he would go through the little door to the telephone and would get instructions and counsel. From the treasure storehouse, he would get seed and all that he needed for each day's work.

So great was Steve's enthusiasm as he saw the garden begin to bloom again, that he would work late and early. One night after dark he stumbled into the porch tired and happy, leaned his shovel against the railing, and fell into the hammock. In a moment he was in dreamland.

The next morning, when Steve woke to the singing of the birds, he was startled to realize that the sun was already high above the horizon. He jumped out of the hammock, grabbed the shovel, and hastened out to the part of the garden in which he had been working the night before.

He set to work with his usual fervor but was surprised to find that the soft, fertile earth no longer yielded to his efforts. He lifted the shovel, and then almost cried as he saw the beautiful rose bush that he had been carefully cherishing fall to the ground, cut off by a careless stroke of the shovel.

Suddenly, amid his frustration Steve heard a voice that sounded with odd, through familiar, discord, "My, but you're working hard," said the salesman from atop the wall.

Steve took one look. In an instant there came over him with a shock the realization of what had happened. He hurled the shovel at the man with all his might and turned and ran as fast as his legs could carry him toward the little door.

Day after day the struggle continued just that way. Whenever he spent time at the telephone and in the storehouse, his work progressed, but always there was something inside of Steve that made him want to skip the little door. Sometimes he even felt a craving for the old fruit—but this was only when he had failed to go through the little door.

Days turned into years, and Steve's joy in the development of the garden was greater and deeper as time went by. Gradually, as he matured, he learned more and more of obedience and faithfulness.

Then came the day, after many years, when Steve rejoiced to view the very last corner of the garden planted, cultivated, and luxuriant in full bloom. And that very same day something happened that never happened since the day Steve had come to the garden.

The telephone rang.

Steve went through the little door, answered the telephone, and heard the voice of the owner of the garden, "You have done well, my son, and you have been faithful. Now come and serve me in my own house forever."

CAMPFIRE

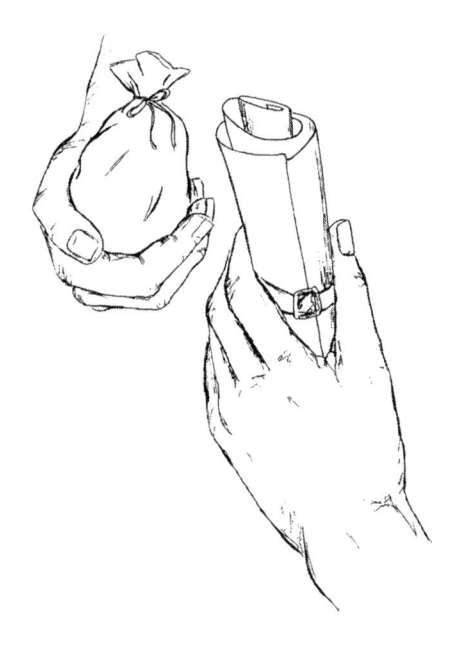

"In consternation Carlo pushed his hand into the bag which he held. In it he had several handfuls of corn."

•••

"In her hand she held a letter. Michael's heart leaped within him as he saw the king's own seal on the letter."

CAMPFIRE

THE CROWNING OF THE KING

From his early youth the prince was loved by all the people of the realm. When the day of his ascent to the throne was announced, all the people of the nation rejoiced. There was much excitement as every man talked with his neighbor about the coming day of their king's coronation.

"It is said that he will go through all of the great highways of the country and talk with everyone along the way. He will ride his great golden chariot. Before him will come all of the courtiers and the members of his court." Indeed, there was much excitement.

Among those who looked forward to the day of the coronation were two men of whom I want to tell you. One was a very young boy named Michael, who lived with his widowed mother and two little sisters. The family depended upon him for their substance. He would go out from day to day to find work he could do, either in the field or in the village. All who hired him found he was honest and fair—a hard worker, but very young. There was another man who lived in that very same village whose name was Carlo. Carlo was a carpenter by trade, but never a very good man because he was lazy. He always sought to find a way to earn without working. It was his belief that a man who was clever enough could get rich without working. When Carlo heard of the coming coronation day, an idea came into his mind.

"Ah, it is well known," he said to himself, "that when the king comes to be crowned, he will give gifts to all the people in the realm, and especially to the poor and needy. I will make myself a poor, wretched cripple, and certainly the king will have mercy upon me, and perchance he will give me a great gift."

When Michael heard, his thoughts were along a different line. "Ah," he said, "the king will come, and I will see him, and perhaps he will come close enough that I will be able to touch his hand. How wonderful it would be to serve the king in his very presence!" He was thinking of those whose privilege it was to serve the king as pages, or as knights, or as courtiers in the very court of the great king.

As the time approached, Carlo, the lazy carpenter, made his preparation. He put on old, worn clothing and put dirty, ragged bandages on his head and limbs. He practiced a limp to seem to be severely afflicted. When the big day came, he went with the crowd to the edge of the highway and awaited the king's coming with his train. Michael stood not far from Carlo, barefoot, for he owned no shoes. His clothes indeed were well-worn, but they were clean and well-patched by his industrious mother. As he stood looking up along the highway, he could see the parade coming.

First, he saw the pages leading the procession - young men dressed in the finery of the king's court, declaring to all the people, "Here comes the king!" Right behind them came the heralds, a bit older, each one with his long silver trumpet, with the banners of the king attached and waving. They sounded as they came, "Ta-ta-Ta—Hear Ye, hear ye, here comes the great king. The king of our nation."

Behind the heralds and in greater splendor came the knights in shining armor astride prancing horses. Their shields were polished mirrors. Their steeds stepped proudly, lifting their hoofs high. Oh, what splendid horses they were with trappings of silver, gold, and purple shone in the brilliant sunlight!

Behind the knights rode the princes themselves. Those who ate at the very table of the king. Then, in the distance behind them, all those who stood by the wayside could see the chariot of the king himself. Much larger were these horses than those which the knights had ridden. High, proud, black, shinning steads, with sparkling harnesses, drew the beautiful chariot. It was the chariot of state, which was used only by the king himself.

But the king was not riding in the chariot. No, earlier in the day he had caused the chariot to stop and he had descended. Now he walked before the horses. As he walked, he would stop and converse with this person or that. He would pat a child upon the head, then talk with a poor widow or beggar here and there along the way. As the king came to the place where Carlo stood, the false beggar pushed his way out into the middle of the street and held his hand up toward the monarch and said, "Ah, Sire, I am a miserable pauper, have mercy upon me."

The king stopped and looked down on the miserable man before him. Looking

CAMPFIRE

into the man's eyes he said, "My son, what will you give to me, on this, my coronation day?"

Carlo looked up in astonishment at the king, "I, give to thee, Sire? Can you not see that I am poor, weak, miserable? What can I have to give to you?"

The king answered only by asking the same question again, and looking deep into the eyes of the man, "What will you give me? This is the day of my coronation as your king. What will you give me?"

In consternation Carlo pushed his hand into the bag which he held. In it he had several handfuls of corn. From this, according to his miserly ways, he withdrew only three kernels. He held them out, his hand trembling, and dropped them into the palm of the king's outstretched hand.

Receiving the three kernels of corn, the king looked down into the man's eyes and said, "Thank you, son. I thank you."

Then the king went his way.

Angered at the failure of his plan, Carlo turned and stamped off toward his home.

A few moments later the king came to the place where Michael stood, wide-eyed and open-mouthed. How beautiful had been the glory of all that he had seen! Michael's eyes lit up at all that he saw coming toward him along the highway. How splendid they appeared! He could see that some of the pages were about his own age and some even younger. How well-fed they must be! How strong, agile, and alert they seemed to be! How wonderful it must be to serve the king!

Then, as he watched, he saw the heralds come with their shinning trumpets, "Ta-ta-Ta—Hear ye, Hear ye!" Oh, how wonderful it would be to announce the coming of the king, wherever he might be! Then, behind them, Michael saw the knights in their shining armor, mounted upon their shinning steads. Oh, how wonderful it must be to be a knight! To do battle for the great king! Then he saw the princes, the wise ones who were accorded the privilege of sitting at the king's own table and eating the king's own meat. The greatest thrill of all for Michael was when the king himself appeared.

As the king came to where the boy stood, he looked into his eyes and repeated the same question that he had asked of Carlo, the false beggar, "My son, what have you for me? What will you give me, on this, my coronation day?"

To hear the voice of the king, looking at him and talking to him, caused Michael's heart to thrill with joy but also with fear.

"I, give to you, Sire?" His hands fell down to his side. "I have nothing, Sire. All

THE CROWNING OF THE KING

that I have is myself." He held up his empty hands. "But, Sire, I will give myself to thee."

Looking down with kind eyes into Michael's own and into the very heart of the boy, the king replied, "Thank you, my son, thank you."

Puzzled, the boy watched the last of the train disappear down the highway, then turned and walked slowly toward his home.

As he came to Carlo's house, he saw the man standing in the doorway. When he had greeted him, Carlo replied with a growl, "All that work, and the king gave me nothing."

With this, Carlo threw the sack which held the corn on the table. Michael, standing in the doorway was amazed to see a glimmer of shinning gold from the table. Carlo saw it too and sprang to look. There, among the kernels of corn, shown three coins of solid gold, resplendent among the corn.

The carpenter looked up in amazement. "Three kernels of corn I gave to the king, and look, he has given me three gold coins. Ah, would that I had given him all my corn!"

The man sank down to his bench and held his head in his hands, full of remorse that he had given so little to the king.

Thinking deep thoughts, Michael continued on his homeward way. As he approached the cottage in which he lived, his mother rushed out to him. In her hand she held a letter. Michael's heart leaped within him as he saw the king's own seal on the letter. Opening it quickly, Michael read a summons signed by the king's own hand. It called him to come to the court to serve the king in his very presence, to eat at the king's table, and to be one of those who bear the name of the king and do his work!

CAMPFIRE

LEGEND OF THE COTTONWOODS

One day in the early spring many years ago, the old Indian chief, White Fox, summoned his sons to the council fire. The boys responded eagerly, for they had been anxiously awaiting his call. White Fox had led his people wisely for many years, but now the time had come for him to face the difficult decision as to which of his twin sons, Straight Arrow or Brave Hawk, would succeed him as chief.

The firelight shone on his leathery face as he said solemnly, "My sons, it is my task to choose which of you will take my place as chief when I am no longer able to be a leader. I cannot make my choice until you have both proven yourselves—as hunters, warriors, and horsemen. My decision will be made known on the day your years number eighteen."

Then, just as Straight Arrow and Brave Hawk were turning away, their father reached under a pile of deer hides beside him and drew out two small saplings. He held them out to the boys and said, "It is my wish that each of you plant one of these small cottonwood trees."

When the boys had left the council fire, Brave Hawk turned to Straight Arrow and said boastfully, "Well, my brother, do you want to give up now? I shall outshoot you, outride you and prove myself to be a more able warrior!" He shook his fist defiantly, still clutching the cottonwood twig.

Straight Arrow smiled at his brother and said, "We shall see, we shall see. Where will you plant your tree?"

Brave Hawk answered in disgust, "What a waste of time! What do I care about planting a scrawny little stick!" Then a sly look crossed his face as he said, "My brother, where have you thought to plant your tree?"

Straight Arrow answered slowly, "Why, I thought, perhaps, in the field about the river—"

Brave Hawk broke in quickly, "Of course, I know the spot, on the edge of the bank, where all the world can see. I'll plant mine right now!" Without a backward glance, he leaped on his horse and galloped off.

Straight Arrow was tempted to follow, but instead, he sought out his old friend Brown Beaver to ask his advice. Brown Beaver knew much about the planting and caring for crops.

Later that afternoon, Straight Arrow set out for the hillside he had mentioned to his brother. He looked first for Brave Hawk's tree and found it several feet from the edge of the rocky cliff. The little tree stood straight and alone, sure to catch the eye of any passerby.

Then Straight Arrow turned his horse and rode to the center of the grassy field several hundred yards away and dismounted. He worked diligently for some time, not only digging a deep hole in which to plant the tree but also clearing away the grass from an area several feet around the hole. When he was finished planting the tree, he made a trip on foot down the rocky trail to the river and returned with a buffalo-hide bag full of water. He poured the water around the little twig, then stood back and surveyed his work.

All through the summer, Straight Arrow cared for his tree with tenderness. He watered it from the river when the skies sent no rain, and he kept the earth around it free from growth. He occasionally glanced toward his brother's tree, which stood on the edge of the river bank. Brave Hawk was so busy training himself for the approaching contents between the two that he didn't have much time to care for his twig, even when a small landslide left some of the young tree's roots exposed.

In the two years that passed before the twins' 18th birthday, White Fox gave them many tests of bravery and skill. Straight Arrow proved himself to be the more skillful hunter, while Brave Hawk won the honors in horsemanship.

On one occasion a nearby tribe went on the warpath. White Fox ordered his sons to go with the war party to meet the attacking tribe. The villagers waited anxiously for news of the chief's sons' conduct in battle. At the sound of approaching horses, the people rushed out to meet the returning warriors. They gasped when they saw the wound on the side of Straight Arrow's head.

Brave Hawk wore a triumphant air as he jumped from his horse and proudly said, "We have driven back our enemies, my father, and I have escaped injury!" He paused and added with obvious difficulty, "But Straight Arrow saved my life, Father. It was because of me that he was hurt."

So it appeared that each son had distinguished himself in battle. They seemed to be evenly matched. How would White Fox be able to decide between his sons? Many of the old chief's advisors confessed they were glad that this was not their decision to make.

At last the boys' eighteenth birthday arrived. Everyone in the Indian village wore the ceremonial dress for the occasion. When all the tribe was assembled, White Fox stepped from his teepee and motioned for his people to follow him. With mounting curiosity, they followed as he led them to the rocky knoll overlooking the river.

There he stopped and said solemnly, "A chief must have many qualities. Some are seen easily with the eyes, such as good horsemanship, hunting skill and bravery in battle. Both of my sons have shown that they possess these qualities. There are other things, however, that a great chief must have. Anyone can plant a tree, but not every man knows how to care for it with wisdom, patience, and love. I gave each of my sons a tree to plant many moons ago. Today you see with your own eyes the results."

He paused and pointed toward the edge of the bank. "Brave Hawk's tree stands alive, but because it was planted in a poor location and uncared for, it is dwarfed and will never grow tall." He then turned and pointed toward the tree in the meadow. "Straight Arrow's tree stands erect, with new growth, pointing to the sky. It will someday become a great tree, under whose shade men can rest in years to come."

The wise old chief came forward and, touching Straight Arrow's shoulder, said proudly, "I choose Straight Arrow to be your new chief. May you, my son, lead our people happily and show them the love and concern which you have shown this little cottonwood tree."

"The emperor ordered the wrestlers to be transported to the icy mountain peaks and marched out on a frozen lake."

CAMPFIRE

FORTY ROMAN WRESTLERS

The well-trained and disciplined army was the backbone of the Roman Empire. One of the many elite fighting units of the Roman army was the group known as the Roman Wrestlers. During times of peace, the wrestlers trained in Rome and put on the exhibitions of wrestling and fighting skills. This group of forty men was the pride of Rome and the Roman army. Beyond this, the Roman Wrestlers were unique because they were all Christians.

In a large empire periods of peace are few and far between. The emperor would often send the Roman Wrestlers to pockets of serious conflict. The presence of the wrestlers would encourage the soldiers of Rome as the wrestlers led them in battle.

The emperor sent the wrestlers to an eastern province where some religious fanatics had started an uprising. Led by the Roman Wrestlers, it didn't take long for the army to quell the rebellion.

The emperor didn't want these eastern fanatics to use their god as a reason to revolt again. So, the emperor had a statue of himself placed in every town in the eastern province. In addition, the emperor decreed that as a symbol of this lordship and deity, every person in every town of the province would have to bow before his statue. To ensure obedience, the emperor threatened to kill any who refused to bow.

FORTY ROMAN WRESTLERS

The emperor had forgotten about the forty Christian wrestlers in the eastern province. When the day came for all to pass by the statue and bow, everyone wondered what the Roman Wrestlers would do.

The line of people moved slowly, bowing as they passed the statue. Those who refused to bow were killed by the sword, on the spot. Eventually the wrestlers moved to the statue. They did not bow, but marched by the statue chanting in unison this refrain,

"Forty Roman Wrestlers we
Marching on for Christ our King!
To win for you the Victory
And from you, the victor's crown."

The soldiers and authorities were no match for the wrestlers. They sent word to the emperor seeking direction.

The wrestlers' sign of defiance angered the emperor. He wanted to make an example of the wrestlers so that no one else would be tempted to disobey him. The emperor ordered the wrestlers to be transported to the icy mountain peaks and marched out on a frozen lake. The wrestlers were to be stripped of clothing and shoes and marched around the lake until they dropped dead.

The emperor provided one means of escape. If a wrestler would recant his faith he could retreat from the lake and bow down to the image of the emperor in the warm guard house nearby and be saved from frozen death.

The march began at midnight. New snow was falling from the sky. The wrestlers rounded the lake many times without showing the effects of the elements. Each time they passed the guard house they repeated the victory chant.

By daybreak, the wrestlers were still circling the lake, but in a struggling, exhausted manner. As they came by the guard house one of the wrestlers broke away from the other thirty-nine and collapsed in the guard house at the feet of the statue. The guard observing this scene was pierced with conviction. The guard dropped his weapons, stripped off his clothes and joined the wrestler ranks.

Spiritually strengthened by this act of faith, the barely living wrestlers repeated their chant one last time. It wasn't long before each and every wrestler fell dead in his tracks.

CAMPFIRE

THE BLACKSMITH

It was a hot, sticky afternoon and Charlie, the popular town blacksmith, was busy working over his forge. He had a big job to complete that day and he didn't let even the heat slow him down.

Outside, the humid air seemed to hang in silent suspense. Suddenly, form not too far away, the silence was pierced with shouts and screams. At first Charlie did not hear it, but soon the noise reached his ears above the sound of his pounding.

Immediately Charlie dropped his hammer and rushed to the door to see what this could be. Then he heard the terrible cry of, "Mad dog! Mad dog!" Without hesitation he hurried into the street.

By this time the people had formed a large circle quite a distance from the dog. Some protected their small children. The commotion was being caused by a small boy who had wandered out in the area near the foaming dog. Terror gripped the crowd as they saw the boy, unaware of his danger, approach the dog, hoping to play with it. Everyone seemed frozen in place.

Charlie quickly took in the situation as he neared the spot. After pausing briefly at the edge of the crown, he suddenly rushed toward the child. Just as the rabid dog turned upon the child, Charlie snatched him up and carried him to the edge of the crown. Charlie could hear the snarling dog close behind and could see the expressions of terror on the faces of the people. Quickly he swung around and

THE BLACKSMITH

faced the dog. Then with his strong arms and hands he grasped by the neck and with great effort was able to strangle it. The crowd cheered him for his heroic deed.

As soon as possible Charlie went back to the shop to get busy with this important job. Now he would probably have to work all night to get finished. As he reached for his hammer he noticed a deep gash on his arm—a bite mark received from the rabid dog. In those days there was no cure for rabies.

Quickly Charlie made a decision. He went across the room and chose a piece of iron. Immediately he started to work. Gradually a chain began to take form.

When he had finished the chain, Charlie left the shop unnoticed. He walked until he reached the woods not far away. He entered the woods alone, found a good spot and then carefully fastened the chain to his wrists and then fastened it to a large tree. Soon the dread effects of rabies would begin to show, and Charlie determined not to endanger anyone when he became violent. When they found his body a few days later, they knew what he had done.

CAMPFIRE

GOLDIE

Goldie had hundreds of acres to roam. She spent hours running over the fields every day, chasing rabbits, squirrels, and anything else that moved. She had virtually no restrictions on what she could do. The one restriction she had was that when her master called, she had to obey and go to him. But this was almost always rewarded with food, a kind word, or a pat on the head. There was nothing that she needed—she had a warm bed, plenty of food, and lots of time to run and play.

One sunny, July afternoon when she was out playing, a rabbit suddenly appeared before her and started running. As she started to chase it, she heard her master call, "Goldie! Come here!!" For the first time in her life, she hesitated and began to wonder why she should go to her master. But the habit was too great, and she turned to go to him. Not long after that, when she was out in the fields, a gopher appeared before her just as her master called. This time she hesitated for a few seconds, and then turned and chased the gopher. She was experiencing something new—freedom.

When she finally returned home late that night, the house was dark. There was no one stirring, and she guiltily climbed onto the steps and went to sleep. It was cold, and without the protection of the house, she shivered all night and got very little sleep. She was also very hungry, because there was no one up to feed her.

The next morning, when her master came out, Goldie stood up and tried her best

GOLDIE

to look sorry for what she had done. Indeed, she was sorry and couldn't believe what she had done. For the next two weeks, she was very good and did everything her master asked.

But then, on another afternoon, once again a rabbit jumped out of the bushes just as her master called. But this time, there was much less hesitation. She almost immediately went and chased the rabbit. Again, she got home really late, but this time, most of the guilt was replaced with a new exhilaration of independence and freedom.

Time went on, and it got so that she didn't even need an excuse when her master called. She just did as she pleased, hardly ever listening to her master. Of course, this upset the master very much, but he loved her so much he did not want to put her on a chain. He kept hoping that she would change her ways and be obedient to him once again.

Then one afternoon, the master took Goldie in the car to town. On the way back, he stopped near a forest to look at a tree that had been struck by lightning. In a flash, Goldie had jumped out of the car to chase a rabbit and was running into the woods. Goldie's master saw her run and started calling to her with fear in his voice because he knew how dangerous the woods were. But Goldie did not listen. She ran deeper and deeper into the woods, suddenly realizing that she was finally free. She did not have to go back to the master. She was on her own. The master finally gave up, and, very sorrowfully, got back in the car and drove home. The next day he went back out to look for her but could not find her.

Winter came, and with it came the cold and the snow. Goldie was struggling to remain alive. There were no longer any rabbits or squirrels to chase for food. Her left front foot had been injured when she got it caught between two dead trees. Her once shiny fur was matted down with mud and brambles. Once a beautiful dog, she now looked like an old stray. She felt the last of her strength leave her body as Goldie curled up beneath a tree.

"Goldie!" she heard from a distance. Goldie perked up her ear but there was only silence. Perhaps it was the sounds of this old woods and her weakened mind playing tricks on her.

"Goldie!" There it was again. This time the sound was much closer. It was the master! He had come for her. Suddenly Goldie strength returned–if only slightly– but it was enough for her to let out a meager yelp.

"Goldie!" she heard the master again. Goldie mustered another bark. Seconds later she felt the warm strong arms of her master wrap around her cold and depleted body. He picked her up and covered her in a wool blanket. Goldie was once again safe in his care and she fell asleep.

CAMPFIRE

Days later, Goldie woke up in a warm home with a cozy bed and plenty of food and water. And there, by her side was the master. He never gave up on Goldie and she knew that she would never ignore his call again.

"Besides its old-west charm, there was something even more unique about the town. The only inhabitants of the town were geese—therefore the name, Goosetown."

CAMPFIRE

GOOSETOWN

The town was located on the valley floor in the western Rockies surrounded by snow-capped mountains. The town looked like it was plucked from an old western movie. The Main Street was lined with wood storefronts, boardwalks, hitching posts, swinging-door saloons, cigar-store Indians, a blacksmith shop with a forge and, of course, like any authentic western town, Main Street was a dusty, unpaved thoroughfare.

Besides its old-west charm, there was something even more unique about the town. The only inhabitants of the town were geese—therefore the name, Goosetown. These were not your barnyard-variety geese. The geese of Goosetown were just like the people of any other community. They ran businesses, raised families and lived stable, productive lives.

Goosetown was a great place to live, except for when it rained. The rain and runoff from the mountains turned Main Street into one giant mud puddle. Every goose in town tracked it everywhere.

This was no small problem for the geese of Goosetown. Every town meeting turned into a lengthy discussion as to what to do about the mud. Each meeting would end with an approved plan of getting rid of the mud.

Every plan worked. The catch was that every time it rained, the mud was back. Rain, mud, meeting, plan, rid of the mud, rain again, mud again, meeting again, plan again, rid of the mud again—the cycle would repeat itself over and over. No one in Goosetown could remember life being any different.

One day the goose pastor was studying the Great Goose Book when he found two pages stuck together. He carefully pulled the pages apart and found some instructions that he'd never seen before. The subtitle of the text was, "A Description of How to Fly."

The goose pastor was most interested. You see, none of the geese of Goosetown could fly. The instructions were simple—bend your knees, flap your wings and push off with your feet. The instructions were so simple that the goose pastor gave them a try. As quick as saying, "One, two, three," the goose pastor was flying around his church study. With the room being too small for developing technique, the pastor perfected the art of flying outside. After soaring, banking and diving through the sky, the goose pastor returned to earth to catch his breath and rest his weary wings.

While thinking of the art of flying, it dawned on the goose pastor that flying was the perfect solution to the mud problem. The geese could just fly over the mud and never get their webbed feet wet. This thought excited the goose pastor so much that he had handbills nailed to every post on Main Street encouraging every goose in Goosetown to attend that Sunday to hear how the mud problem could be solved forever.

The goose pastor's notices caused quite a stir in town and when Sunday arrived, everyone was in church. After the songs, announcements and offering, the goose pastor got up to the pulpit and began to share the "One, Two, Three" method of flying. Everyone caught on right away and began to whisper, 'Great! Awesome! Wonderful! Amazing!" to one another. Because of the enthusiasm, the goose pastor even demonstrated the technique in church. All the geese were flabbergasted. Excitement increased. The pastor was so elated that he had everyone in church try, too. It was some sight to see a church full of geese, each flying above his place in the pew.

By the time the last song was sung and the benediction was spoken, the excitement of the good news was on everyone's lips as they exited the church. All they could think or talk about was the fascinating new knowledge of flight–as each goose walked home, picked up mud in the webbed feet and tracked it back into their homes.

CAMPFIRE

SIR BRIAN'S SHIELD

Adapted from a story by Raymond MacDonald Alden

Long, long ago there was a dark, ancient forest named Drearwood. It was much older and larger than any forest we know of today. In Drearwood there lived a terrible race of giants that preyed upon those brave enough to travel through the forest. Now they had, on occasion, become bold enough to attack the settlements on the edge of that great wood.

In the center of Drearwood rose a high bluff upon which set a bright castle. In that castle lived a group of brave knights whose job it was to protect all those who traveled through or lived near the great forest. Each knight carried a long slender lance, a magical silver shield, and a great red plume which people in distress could see from a great way off.

Long before the time of knights there lived in the castle a great craftsman, a master smith, who made the wonderful silver shields the knights of the castle carried. These shields had magical properties. If a knight were especially brave, loyal, or obedient to his Lord, the Master of the castle, the shield would grow brighter and brighter until it shone so that the knight could see his reflection in it. But if he were cowardly or disobedient it grew dull and gray so that the knight was ashamed to show it in the castle. However, if a knight performed a brave or courageous act in service to the Lord, in the center of his shield appeared a bright golden star that shone as the sun. So far the only person to ever have a golden star appear on his shield was the Lord of the castle.

SIR BRIAN'S SHIELD

One day word came to the Lord of amassing of giants in the Wraithills deep in the darkest center of Drearwood. From there the giants planned to sweep through all the settlements, killing the people then trapping the knights at the fords of Bristol thereby ridding the forest of their enemies forever. The Lord had to meet the giants in battle before this could happen. That battle would be more terrible than nearly all that had come before. It was the first time that the knights had fought against such a large force of giants. Usually the knights only fought against individual giants such as when the Lord of the castle singlehandedly defeated the King of the giants. As you can imagine all the knights were excited and somewhat frightened of the upcoming battle with their greatest foes.

This story deals with one young knight named Sir Brian. He was a brave and noble knight who had helped many travelers through the dark forest, as could be told by his shield being almost bright enough to see his reflection in. He was particularly looking forward to the upcoming battle in which he could perform many great and honorable feats for his Lord.

On the eve of the great battle Sir Brian saw the Lord of the castle walking toward him. He was pleased for he thought the Lord surely had some great task for him to perform. The Lord did have a task for Sir Brian but not the one he had hoped for. Instead, he asked Sir Brian to guard the gates of the castle while he was gone and to allow no one to enter. Sir Brian's heart sank. He had hoped for some great task, not castle sitting. To be appointed steward of the castle gates was a great honor, but Sir Brian wanted to meet the giants in battle. However, he knew it was his Lord's command. He had to obey.

The next morning the knights rode forth against the giants and Sir Brian watched them go down the road until at last even their great red plumes were out of sight.

In the afternoon Sir Brian watched and waited. He could just hear, far off in the distance the sounds of battle. About two hours later, at the edge of the forest, Sir Brian saw something move. When it came closer he saw it was an old woman in beggar's rags. She came up to the castle wall and shouted up to Sir Brian, "Steward of the gates, my village has been overrun by giants. My family is dead and all my belongings are destroyed. Please open the castle gates and allow me to enter in for food and shelter." Sir Brian looked over the castle wall down at the woman.

"I'm sorry old woman. I cannot open the castle gates by the order of the Lord of the castle himself. I can give you some food over the wall and you could stay near the castle wall for safety but I cannot open the gate. It is the Lord's command that the gates not be opened until he returns and I cannot disobey my Master's commands." Sir Brian called a nearby page to run and get the woman some food, then he let it down to the ground on a long cord.

CAMPFIRE

After the old woman had eaten she told Sir Brian that the giants were fighting as never before and that they might defeat the knights, and a fresh knight like himself might turn the tide of battle and win great glory by saving his Lord. At this Sir Brian's eyes brightened because he knew this might be true and would give him a chance to fight the giants like he had wished. But then his shoulders slumped and the brightness left his eyes. His Lord had told him to stay and guard the castle. He was the steward of the castle gates. He knew he could not go. Sir Brian bent over the wall and shouted down to her, "I'm sorry, I must obey my Lord's command. I cannot leave the castle."

"Then you are a coward and unworthy of your shield," the woman shouted back. He knew this was not true but it still hurt him because he did so wish to go into battle. But no, he had to follow the Lord's orders. The woman pestered Sir Brian for some time but eventually she went away, back into the depths of Drearwood. Sir Brian continued to watch the gate and wait for the return of his Lord.

After nearly two hours had passed another figure approached the castle. It was a young knight from the castle named Sir John. Sir John was limping. As he reached the gate he called up to Sir Brian, "Sir Brian, the giants are defeating us. I have come back because I am wounded. Now I may watch the castle and you may go to the battle." At first Sir Brian was glad of this for now he could leave the castle safe in the hands of another knight and go join the battle. But again, his shoulders slumped for he knew he could not go. He alone was told to guard the castle. He told Sir John this and Sir John admitted he was right and went back into the forest holding his head higher and not limping quite so much. Sir Brian was left again to guard the castle. There he waited for five or so more hours while nothing happened.

When it was nearly dark, Sir Brian saw another figure approaching from the shadows of the wood. At first he thought it was a knight because of how the figure carried itself, but when it came closer Sir Brian saw that it was an old man in a dark cloak. He called up to Sir Brian, "I am the master wizard Imreldas. I have come to you Sir Brian from a great distance to bring you this." At this he held up what appeared to be a sword with a beautifully jeweled hilt and sheath.

"It is a magic sword and none can stand against the one who wields it. Your friends are being destroyed by the giants and only you can use this sword to save them," said the wizard. Sir Brian felt he had to take the sword and go rescue the knights and his Lord. He started to run down the stairs to open the gate. When almost at the gate he stopped. His shoulders slumped again. His Lord had told him to stay and guard the castle no matter what. He had to do as he was commanded. Slowly he turned and climbed the stairs.

"I am sorry Master Imreldas. I cannot accept your gift. The Lord of the Castle has commanded me to stay and guard the castle gates and to allow no one to pass through the gates until he has returned. Perhaps the sword can be given to another knight or even to the Lord of the castle himself."

The wizard replied, "This sword will obey only your command Sir Brian for it was long ago forged for your use on this very day."

"I'm sorry," said Sir Brian, "by the Lord's command I must refuse." In anger the wizard threw back his cloak and raised his staff.

"Only a coward would not save his friends when he has been given such an opportunity," he shouted. But Sir Brian was firm and simply said, "I will obey my Lord's command."

Seeing it was useless to argue further, the wizard turned and walked, enraged, into the forest shadows. But as he did a strange thing happened. Instead of growing smaller as he walked away the man grew larger until he was as large as any giant in the forest. The last Sir Brian saw of the giant was his head moving above the treetops in the first light from the moon that evening. Sir Brian leaned against the castle wall and breathed a great sigh of relief. If he had taken the magic sword, which he saw now as only an old stick, and left the castle, the few servants of the Lord that remained in the castle would have been utterly defeated by the giant and the knights would have no safe haven of return, even if they were victorious. That did it for Sir Brian. No matter what else happened, no one would enter the castle, and he would not leave the gate until the Lord himself returned!

The next morning Sir Brian could see the first signs of the returning knights in the early sunlight. First he saw a cloud of dust, then the red plumes. Finally, he saw the dull outlines of the knights returning in the faint light. It looked as if most the knights were there, even Sir John.

After the Lord of the Castle had passed through the gates and all the knights were in, Sir Brian left his post and went down to the great hall of the castle to return the golden keys of the gates to the Lord.

As Sir Brian passed through the city he stopped to hear many of the rumors of the battle and how the giants had run with fear at the sight of the Lord of the castle. Sir Brian was very sad that he had not been there to see the charge of the Lord and the defeat of the giants. But then he remembered the golden keys and his mission. He went on his way.

As Sir Brian entered the great hall he saw all the knights lined up on either side of the hall that led to the Lord's throne. As he walked up to the throne he heard the other knights whispering. He knew the battle must have been great indeed because a knight never spoke in that hall unless the Lord had asked him a question. He was able to hear some of them say, "his shield, look at his shield," as

CAMPFIRE

he passed by. But he dared not turn aside to look. Such an act would show great disrespect to the Lord of the castle.

When he reached the throne he noticed a puzzled look on the Lord's face as the Lord looked into his eyes. Then the Lord asked Sir Brian to give an account of all that had happened that day. Specifically he asked if any giants had attacked the castle. Sir Brian told his Lord everything had happened and that the only giant to come had left when he saw he could not enter the castle. The Lord said "Sir Brian, are you sure no great battle was fought here?" Sir Brian replied, "No my Lord, all that has happened is as I have told you." A puzzled look came over the Lord's face, then He said, "Sir Brian look at your shield." Sir Brian turned and took a sharp breath. For there, in the center of his shield, was a bright golden star. The Lord again asked Sir Brian if there had been a great battle at the castle. Sir Brian turned back and responded, "No, my Lord. I do not understand this." Then the Lord stood and said, "Sir Brian, the silver shields never lie. Your battle today has been to obey the commands of your Lord while guarding the castle gates. A complete victory has been given to you. Well done, my good and faithful servant."

"The princess is inside the cave, but the cave is guarded by a fierce dragon."

CAMPFIRE

ANDY THE DRAGON FIGHTER

by David White

A red-haired boy ran as fast as he could down the street, following the knights as they returned from battle. Andy was a stable boy and needed to take care of the knights' horses. They would be tired and maybe hurt, after returning from whatever adventure the knights had just been on. Andy loved listening to the knights as they spoke to one another at the stable.

As Andy helped take the saddles, stirrups, and armor off of the horses, he eagerly listened to Sir George speak to Sir Henry. "My goodness! What a terrible trip that was! I had no idea it would be that hard. I'm so sad that brave Sir James is dead. We should have listened to that wise old man that said he knew how to rescue the princess."

The princess! Andy's ears burned with even more curiosity as he tried not to stare at the knights. The princess had been kidnapped the week before, and the knights had been sent out to find her and bring her back. The beautiful princess was the pride and joy of her father, the king. She was the only child of the king and queen, and she was heir to the throne of the kingdom. Whoever married her would be the next king of the land, and her father would surely give a huge reward to anyone who was able to save her. Andy had seen her once before, in a parade. She was indeed very beautiful, and Andy wondered how wonderful it could be to rescue her, perhaps winning her heart and becoming her husband and the future king.

ANDY THE DRAGON FIGHTER

The two knights didn't notice the red-headed stable boy as they continued their discussion. Sir Henry was talking. "Yes, we should have listened to the old man. Once we get rested and resupplied, we should go back and find him. Where did we meet him again?"

"We met him in Blackford," Sir George replied.

"Right, right. He was in the little house by the church. What a strange, old man."

Andy wasn't able to hear any more of the conversation as the knights walked away to the barracks, where they would attend to their wounds and prepare to go out again. Still, he didn't need to hear another word. He had heard enough and had already made up his mind. He would go find the old man and then rescue the princess!

As soon as he could, Andy raced home. He threw some food and a blanket in his bag, kissed his mother goodbye, and headed out for the great city to Blackford. He had asked for directions from the gatekeeper, who told him to follow the road south along the coast until he reached a fork in the road. Then he was to turn to the left and continue until he came to an intersection, where he was to turn right. Andy thanked the gatekeeper and headed north on the main road. The gatekeeper saw him making that mistake and told him to go the other way, so he did. After a long day of walking and taking a few wrong turns, Andy finally made it to Blackford.

He asked around about the old man, and sure enough, the old man was in the little house by the church. He wasn't home, though, so Andy leaned against the house, snacked on his food, and soon fell asleep, exhausted from his journey.

He woke up with a start. The old man was standing in front of him, poking him with a cane. It was morning. "Why are you here, son?" the old man asked.

"I want to find and rescue the princess," Andrew declared boldly.

"Well, rescuing the princess is no easy task. A party of knights tried a few days ago but didn't want to hear my advice. If they had let me tell them, they would have known how to rescue that fair maiden."

"How can I save her?" the ambitious red-haired boy spoke.

"Well, first you have to cross the river, a difficult task in itself. To do so, you need to build a raft, and you must only cross the river at Dead Man's Bend, which is ten miles to the south, otherwise, the raging current will tear your raft apart. After you've crossed the river, you must climb up a steep hill to the west. When you do, go straight up. Don't go to the side, even though it looks easier. At the top of the hill is a great plateau that you must cross to get to the princess, but it's a long journey, so take a long drink from the spring at the top of the hill. You must then

CAMPFIRE

head across the plateau toward the big mountain to the west. Before you reach the mountain, there will be a valley—at the bottom there is a cave. The princess is inside the cave, but the cave is guarded by a fierce dragon. Don't worry, though, it is a very sleepy dragon and will stay asleep as long as you sing lullaby—'Twinkle twinkle little star'—as loud as you can. As you walk by, don't look directly at it, because it can tell when someone is watching it."

"Is that all?" Andy asked.

"Is that all?!" the old man replied. "Well, I guess so, but these are very important instructions, and you must follow all of them to reach the princess. I'm a little worried about you, son. Here, let me write these down for you. Before you cross the river, make sure you memorize these instructions, just in case you lose the paper on your journey."

When the old man had given Andy the paper, the boy dashed off towards the river and headed south. As he went, he read the directions several times, trying to commit it to memory. But memorizing was hard and soon he took a break from trying to remember the instructions. He walked on and on and on for miles, but he still had not reached Dead Man's Bend. His legs were tired. He stopped to rest and noticed something—the river flowed towards the south. "It would be a lot easier," Andy thought, "for me to build the raft here and just float down the river to the south until I reach Dean Man's Bend. Then I can cross. The water looks peaceful enough here by the shore. I'll just stay near the bank of the river until I reach the bend." So that is what he did.

By the time Andy had built his raft, it was already getting a little late in the day. Nevertheless, Andy set off in the river to float downstream. He had built a sturdy raft and had a long pole to guide it by. Everything was going smoothly as he casually floated down the river, staying very close to the shore for safety. Everything went fine until he came to a big tree trunk that had fallen into the river long ago. To get around it, Andy had to move farther away from the river bank. The farther he got from the bank, the swifter the river became. Soon, he was unable to control his movement with his pole. The river took over his trip downstream. The water was getting more and more violent and it was all Andy could do to cling onto the raft for dear life. Even as he was doing this, waves washed over him and the boat, soaking him and his clothes and his bag and his things. Andy couldn't tell how long he struggled on the raft. Each second felt like a hundred years. Very soon, though, Andy's raft hit a big rock and was dashed to pieces. Andy was cast into the river and struggled to stay afloat. He couldn't struggle forever, though, and eventually, everything went black.

Andy woke up to the sound of the raging river. He had washed up on the rivers' edge and had been unconscious for who knows how long. As he slowly stood up, he tried to figure out where he was. As he looked around, he was delighted to discover that he had made it to the other side of the river. Even better than that, as he looked at the river, it seemed that he was at Dead Man's Bend! He turned around. There was the steep hill he had to climb! He was exactly where he needed to be!

"Wow, that was lucky," Andy thought. He had indeed made it across the river alive and was at the right spot, but all his things were soaked. His food was soggy and the directions the old man had written down were all smudged and hard to read. Andy went carefully over the directions, trying to remember the parts that he couldn't read. Then, turning to the west, he confidently continued on his journey.

When he came to the hill, Andy started going straight up, just as the old man had said. But it was very hard, and he tired quickly. The way to the side looked so much easier and there was a clear path that plenty of other people had taken before, so he went that way. Several hours later, he made it to the top of the hill. He was tired, and it was late, but before he stopped to sleep for the night, he looked down the steep hill. From his position at the top of the hill, he could see that the path straight up was clearly the better way to go. Sure, it was harder, but he would have made it up the hill much sooner. "Oh, well," the boy thought. "At least I made it up here. I've got a big day ahead of me tomorrow, rescuing the princess and all. I better get my beauty sleep." Exhausted and tired, after he drank from a nearby spring and tried to eat his food, he went to sleep.

In the morning, he looked at and tried to remember the directions again. He went over to the spring to get a nice long drink before his journey. "Ew! Yuck! This water is disgusting!" Andy exclaimed. The water did not taste as good as it had the night before after he was exhausted from his ordeal the day before. As every hiker knows, just about any cold drink can taste good after a long hike. Andy tried to drink the water, but it was just so gross. After a few sips, he decided that was enough. He gazed off into the western horizon and saw the distant mountain showing him which way to head.

Off he went, marching across the great open plateau. The morning was cool, the birds were chirping, and the princess was on the boy's mind. He dreamed of the look on the maiden's face as he strode bravely and handsomely into the cave and revealed himself as her rescuer. He dreamed of the reception he would receive as he returned triumphantly into the capital city with the princess. He dreamed of the great reward the king would give to him, perhaps making him a knight or letting him marry the princess—or both! His dreams trailed off after a while, as the hot noonday sun beat down on him. He walked on in the heat of the afternoon and grew tired quickly. When the day was hot, he was sweating profusely, but soon he was sweating less and less. He just didn't have as much moisture in his

CAMPFIRE

body to sweat anymore. Nevertheless, he plodded on, one foot in front of the other, marching flatly across the plateau, wanting to win his prize—the princess.

He wasn't even thinking about the steps he was taking when he suddenly took a step downward. A step down? He now became aware of his surroundings. He looked. There before him lay the valley. He strained his eyes and looked at the valley's bottom, but he could not see the cave—or the dragon. He did notice, however, a stream at the bottom of the valley. But it was getting late. There were only a few more hours of daylight. Should he continue into this unknown valley, with a dragon somewhere in it? Or should he rest where he was and wait for morning. As he considered his predicament, all he could think about was nice, cold water. So, he mustered the little bit of energy he had left and continued, stumbling down into the valley.

After an hour, he had made it to the bottom and drank deeply from the stream at its base. When he had quenched his deep thirst, he looked around. Down the valley, about a half-mile away, was the cave. It was a huge cave, invisible from above the valley, but obvious from within it. Andy looked carefully and thought he could make out the massive hulk of the dragon's body at the mouth of the cave. Mustering all his courage and what little strength he had left, he walked toward the cave.

As he got closer, he could clearly see the dragon in the evening light. The dragon was sleeping! The dragon's sides went up and down as it took the deep breaths of deep, sound sleep. Little bits of smoke puffed out of its nostrils with each breath. Andy was so excited. He could just sneak past the dragon while it was sleeping! But something stopped him. He remembered that the old man had told him something about the dragon. Something about sleeping and singing and—something else. Andy took out the instructions the old man had written down. He tried to read them, but the washed away words and the dim light made reading difficult. He suddenly had a flash of memory, though, and remembered that the old man had said to sing "Twinkle, twinkle, little star" as loud as he could as he went by the dragon, so the dragon would sleep, and not to look at the dragon for some reason or another.

But in Andy's present situation, those instructions didn't seem to make sense. The dragon was already asleep, so why would you need to sing him a lullaby? And who in their right mind would not look at a dragon, especially if it were sleeping? How would you know if it would wake up or not? And what did some old man who lived next to the church in Blackford know about dragons anyway? Maybe Andy remembered the instructions wrong. Andy could not understand how those silly directions would apply in this situation. It just didn't make sense. He put the directions back in his bag and set it aside.

ANDY THE DRAGON FIGHTER

Andy looked at the cave. Somewhere in that cave was his lovely princess, just waiting to be rescued. That thought gave him courage and confidence. He was the man to rescue the damsel. He could do it. He knew it. He was a good brave guy, and his time had come. So, very quietly, Andy crawled out from his hiding place about a hundred yards from the cave's mouth. He snuck forward, careful not to make any sound over the shifting pebbles. A smile crept across his face. He was doing it. He glanced over to the dragon. Its sides were still going up and down and little puffs of smoke were coming from its snout. His eyes shot back to the log across which he was walking. It was tough to keep his balance. When he regained his balance, he looked back at the place the dragon was sleeping.

It wasn't asleep anymore. The dragon's eyes were open, and the dragon was looking right back at him.

Needless to say, Andy did not rescue the princess. In fact, no one ever heard from Andy the red-haired stable-boy again. When the knights came the next day, singing "Twinkle, twinkle, little star," they found and rescued the princess. They also found a bag with some moldy food and some directions that had been smeared by water—unheeded wisdom that had been tossed aside and ignored.

CAMPFIRE

THE WIDOW'S SON

by Peter Westerman

There once was a widow who lived with her son on a farm. This land was their way of life for years, growing crops that supplied them with grain that they would use to make bread and sell in the market. The king of this land was a great and noble leader and loved dearly by all of his subjects.

However, there came a time where the rain did not fall. Three years passed without a single cloud in the sky. The widow and her son could grow no crops, and their storehouses slowly dwindled to nothing.

"My son, I fear for our lives. If the rains do not return, we shall surely die," the widow explained to her son.

"What shall we do? There must be some way for us to survive!" answered the son with desperation.

The widow sat in silence for a few moments, and then lifting her eyes, said to her son, "Perhaps the king will help us. My boy, gather some traveling supplies and go see if you can present a plea to his majesty."

Gathering a satchel and filling it with a small portion of food and water, the widow's son set off to speak with the king. It was a long and treacherous voyage, encompassing many days. When the boy finally made it to the castle he had run out of water and food and was on the brink of starvation.

He approached the gate and called up to the guard, "Please, sir! Allow me to

THE WIDOW'S SON

enter the castle. I must speak with the king!"

"What business do you have with the king, little boy?" inquired the guard.

"I come on behalf of my widowed mother, we own a farm out in the countryside but with this drought we have run out of food and will surely starve," cried the boy.

"The whole kingdom suffers, but come in and plead your case to the king. Perhaps he will find mercy on you and your mother." With that, the guard opened the gate and the widow's son entered the castle.

Inside the walls, the castle appeared to be carrying on as usual. One would not know that the whole kingdom was suffering from a drought. Walking through the market place, the boy stared with large eyes at the full carts of fruits and vegetables that were for sale. His mouth water and he could feel his stomach begin to ache with hunger.

He continued towards the king's court. Upon arriving, he was greeted by another guard. "I wish to speak with the king," the boy explained.

"I am sorry my little friend, but the king is very busy today. Come back tomorrow and try again," the guard turned and looked away.

"No, you don't understand. I came from very far away. My mother and I are out of food and will surely starve. I came to beg the king for food so that we might live," the young boy was on the brink of tears.

The guard looked back at the boy and saw how desperate he was, and then said, "You cannot see the king today, but perhaps one of his ambassadors will speak with you. Enter and I will take you to one."

The door swung open and the boy entered into the king's courtroom. There stood the guard, beckoning with his hand for the boy to follow him. He walked behind the guard who led him into a side room. Sitting in a chair facing a window was an older man who was wearing an exquisite robe.

"Ehh hmm" the guard cleared his throat in an attempt to get the old man's attention.

Turning around to face the two who were standing in the door, the man said, "Oh why hello there, how may I help you?"

The guard stepped forward saying, "this young man has traveled a great distance and has a request for you. I leave him in your company." The guard whirled around and walked out of the room.

"Please, have a seat and make yourself comfortable. What is it that you wish to ask of me?" said the old man.

CAMPFIRE

"We have no food left because of this drought. Please, would the king be able to provide for us out of his storehouses so that my me and my mother might live?" pleaded the boy.

"Surely you must have some food remaining," insisted the old man, "tell me, how much do you have left?"

"I have not been home in a few days, but when I left there were only handfuls of flour and a jug of oil that was almost empty," he explained. "If I return home without any more food, we can only hope that my mother can use what's left to prepare one last meal to share before we die."

"Hmm I see. Well it sounds as if your situation is truly dire. Allow me to consult the king personally, and see what can be done." The old man was gone only a moment before returning to the chamber. "Do not fear! The king has instructed me to return to your household and do as you have said—we will use the remaining flour and oil to make a meal for you and your mother."

"Huh?—" the boy began to question, but the king's ambassador continued.

"—But first, let us make a little cake out of it for me. For the king has declared, 'the jar of flour will not empty and the jar of oil will not dry until rain returns to the land.'" After saying these things, the old man gathered his robe, and moved towards the door.

The boy didn't know what to do but to follow. Thoughts and concerns flew through his mind, but he voiced none of them. The old man was moving so quickly that his tired legs had a hard time keeping up with him. Together they left the castle and began venturing off back towards the boy's home. *How does he even know where I live?* The boy thought, but the old man kept walking as if he was being led.

They walked for days without ceasing and made it back to the boy's home in half the time it took his original journey. The young boy was exhausted, collapsing just as he caught view of his house. He saw the old man's face leaning over him, and then—black.

The boy awoke to the sound of laughter. At first everything was blurry, but slowly he regained his vision and could see the old man and his mother sitting next to his bed. They were both staring at him with smiles across their faces.

"Wha... what happened?" the boy struggled to speak.

"My son! It was an absolute miracle. I saw this man carrying you in his arms. He came right into the house without explaining a thing. He took you upstairs, laying you out on the bed. Then he started praying. He cried out to his Lord asking him to save you! I rushed over to your side, and son, you were not breathing! I thought you were dead. But then after the third time this man prayed, you started breathing again!" the widow began to weep with joy.

"After that," the widow continued, "he told me to make some bread. I explained that we only had enough for one more loaf of bread, but he promised me there would be enough. Son, the jars are full and they won't empty! Every time I pour from them, there is always more left."

The old man sat there smiling, eating some bread. He broke off a piece and handed some to the boy. "Please my child, eat up and regain your strength. There is plenty more where this came from."

CAMPFIRE

NEW RAGS FOR OLD

Adapted from a story by Walter Wangerin Jr.

Early before dawn one Friday morning, I noticed a young man handsome and strong walking down the alleys of our city. He was pulling a cart filled with clothes bright and new, calling in a clear voice, "Rags! Rags! New rags for old! I'll take your tired rags!" This was a wonder. The man stood six feet four, arms like tree trunks, hard and muscular, and his eyes flashed intelligence. Could he find no better job than this, a Ragman in the inner city? I followed him. My curiosity drove me. I wasn't disappointed. Soon the Ragman saw a young woman sitting on her back doorstep. She was sobbing into a handkerchief, sighing and shedding a thousand tears. Her shoulder shook. Her heart was breaking. The Ragman stopped his cart.

Quietly, he walked to the women, stepping around the tin cans, dead toys and rubbish. "Give me your rag," he said so gently, "and I'll give you another" He slipped the handkerchief from her eyes. She looked up and he laid across her palm a linen cloth so clean and new that it shone. She blinked from the gift to the giver.

Then as he began to pull the cart again, the Ragman did a strange thing. He put her stained handkerchief to his own face and then he began to weep, to sob as grievously as she had done, his shoulders shaking. Yet she was left without a tear.

This is a wonder, I breathed to myself, and I followed the sobbing Ragman like a child who cannot turn away from the mystery. "Rags! Rags! New rags for old!"

In a little while, as the evening drew in, the Ragman came upon a girl whose head was wrapped in a bandage, whose eyes were empty. Blood soaked her bandage. A single line of blood ran down her cheek. Now the Ragman looked upon the child with pity and drew a lovely yellow bonnet from his cart.

"Give me your rags," he said, tracing his own line on her cheek, "and I'll give you mine." The child could only gaze at him while he loosened the bandage, removed it, and tied it on his own head. The bonnet he set on hers. And I gasped at what I saw.

For with the bandage, went the wound! Against his brow ran a darker, more substantial blood, his own!

"Rags! Rags! I take old rags!" cried the sobbing, bleeding, strong, intelligent Ragman.

The Ragman seemed more and more now to hurry. "Are you going to work?" he asked a man who leaned against a telephone pole. The man shook his head. The Ragman pressed him. "Do you have a job?" "Are you crazy?" sneered the other.

He pulled away from the pole, revealing the right sleeve of his jacket-flat, the cuff stuffed into his pocket. He had no arm.

"So," said the Ragman, "give me your jacket, and I'll give you mine." Such quiet authority in his voice. The one-armed man took off his jacket. So did the Ragman—and I trembled at what I saw. The Ragman's arm stayed in the sleeve, and when the other put it on, he had two good arms, strong as tree trunks, but the Ragman had only one.

"Go to work," he said. After that he found a drunk, lying unconscious, beneath an army blanket, an old man, hunched and wizened and sick. He took the blanket and wrapped it around himself, but for the drunk he left new clothes.

And now I had to run to keep up with the Ragman, though he was weeping uncontrollably and bleeding freely at the forehead, pulling his cart with one arm and stumbling for drunkenness, falling again and again, exhausted, old and sick—yet he went with terrible speed.

On spider's legs he skittered through the alleys of the city, this mile and the next, until he came to its limits and then he rushed beyond. I wept to see the change in this man. I hurt to see his sorrow. And yet I needed to see where he was going in such haste, perhaps even to discover what drove him so.

The little old Ragman—he finally came to a landfill. He went to the garbage pits. And then I wanted to help him in what he did, but I hung back, hiding. He climbed a hill. With tormented labor, he cleared a little space on that hill. Then he sighed. He lay down. He pillowed his head on a handkerchief and a jacket. He covered his bones with an army jacket. And then he died.

CAMPFIRE

Oh, how I cried to witness that death! I slumped in a junked car and wailed and mourned as one who has no hope because I had come to love the Ragman. I sobbed myself to sleep. I did not know—how could I know?—that I slept through Friday night and Saturday and its night too. But then on Sunday I was awakened by a violent light.

Light—pure, hard, demanding light—slammed against my sleeping face and I blinked and looked, and I saw the last and first wonder of all.

The Ragman was folding the blanket most carefully, a scar on his forehead but alive! And besides that, so healthy! There was no sign of sorrow, or of age and all the rags he had shined for cleanliness.

Well I lowered my head and trembling for all that I had seen. I got out of the junk car and walked to the Ragman. I told him my name with shame, for I was a sorry figure next to him. Then I stripped myself of everything and I said to him with yearning in my voice,

"Dress me. Make me new again!" He dressed me—my Lord! He put new rags on me and I am a wonder beside Him.

The Ragman! The Ragman! The Christ!

"With his arm in agony, and with every ounce of strength that he possessed, he reached for the pack which only moments before had been his pillow."

CAMPFIRE

THE SILVER ORB

by Donald Smith

Garen was chosen by the King to fulfill a quest—to confront and defeat the dragons that had invaded the land. He was given a special weapon—a silver orb of living light. To use this weapon, he had to do just two things: be in the presence of evil and call on the name of the Most High trusting in His power.

It had been a long journey. He had been pressing on for weeks. He was tired of the brush and the wilderness. But he continued to press ahead. He followed the orb at first, but after a while, tired of it. So, he bundled it up in some cloth and kept it wrapped in his pack. And, after a while, he forgot about it. He should not have done that.

He was hungry. It had been days since he had seen anyone to get food from. There did not seem to be any game to hunt. The old and flat bread that he carried was molding. Even the cheese that he carried had become rancid, so he discarded it days earlier.

He came to a little clearing atop the mountain that he needed to go over to get to the country in the north where he was instructed to go. It was getting colder. He stopped in a little depression that was out of the wind to make his camp for the night. He was alone.

With his flint and steel, he was able to start a small fire. He warmed himself and was beginning to feel a little bit lonely when he heard something.

THE SILVER ORB

He drew his small sword and expected something fierce to come charging out of the bushes but instead was surprised to see a small—

"What is that?" He wondered.

It was small and covered with short, smooth, metallic-blue fur. It had big black eyes, and two large, ridiculous looking, floppy ears and a long sleek tail. It was almost comical in appearance.

He hopped out of the bushes and came right near the fire. "What are you?" Garen said to himself, but the small animal answered him.

"If you don't like my colors, I can change them." The small animal shook his fur, and instantly, he was burnt orange in color. He shook again, and he was yellow with pink stripes. He shook once again and was the deepest of forest green.

"What are you?" Garen asked as he sheathed his sword. He had never seen a small animal like this before.

"I am happiness. I am joy. I am anything that your heart desires, because, well—I am. But at this moment, I am cold. May I sit by your fire?"

Garen cautiously welcomed the little animal to sit by the fire. For the time being, he would appreciate the company. He was tired, hungry, and feeling so alone.

The little animal came right next to him, and Garen, startled by the forwardness of the animal, began to get to his feet.

"Oh sit—sit—sit—I'm not going to bite you. Just sit." It said.

So Garen sat.

The little animal spoke. "I live here, and I have never seen your kind before. What are you?"

"I'm a man," replied Garen.

"What are you doing here?"

"I'm on a quest."

"A quest? That sounds important. What kind of quest?"

Feeling more secure, Garen began to brag. "The King has given me the task of destroying the dragons in the land."

"Dragons?! Exclaimed the little animal. His body language was tense, and he walked in small circles. "What have the dragons done to make you so angry at them?"

"Oh. I'm not angry. I've been chosen to carry the orb. I've been chosen to slay them. I just need to take the orb and call on the name of the Most High God, and

CAMPFIRE

they'll be slain."

"But why?" asked the little animal in its most timid tone.

"Because dragons are evil," Garen explained. "They kill. They maim. They deceive and destroy. They twist what is natural into something hideous. They are deceiving people into revolting against the King."

"Oh! They sound frightful." Exclaimed the shivering animal.

"Don't worry. I'll protect you. I have my sword, and the orb and nothing will harm you tonight."

"Are you sure we're safe—from dragons?"

"Positive," said Garen.

The little animal moved right against Garen's leg. He could feel the warmth of its body, and he could feel its soft, smooth fur, and he liked the feel.

Into the night they chatted. The animal asked more and more questions about Garen, and he complimented the knight on his bravery.

Garen really liked the little green fuzzball. After a while, and without realizing it, he reached out and began to gently pet the little animal's soft red fur and began to think about going home.

Hungry and tired, Garen no longer felt alone. He felt like he had found a new friend.

He told the little animal all about his home, his mission, and the King that he served. The little animal listened with great interest. Occasionally the little animal would ask things like, "How do you know you can trust the King? And what if the stories he heard about the dragons were wrong, and the dragons were really friendly?" More than once he asked, "What if you fail in your quest?"

Garen would reply, "I won't fail. I've been chosen. I have the orb."

The little animal asked, "If a dragon were here right now—would you slay it?"

"Of course I would," was Garen's honest reply.

Late into the night, when darkness was the blackest, the little animal turned to Garen and asked, "Are you my friend?"

"I guess so," answered Garen.

"I'm so glad," the little animal responded. Then he curled into a small ball and fell fast asleep.

Leaning against a rock, Garen tucked his backpack behind his head and used it for a pillow. For a time, he stroked the animal's soft fur. Then he too began to doze and soon fell into a deep sleep.

After several hours, the little animal awakened from its sleep. He got up and moved silently away from Garen without as much as a sound. He walked just beyond the dying fire, and with his head bent low, and he began to stretch. As his head came up, and with his arms stretched above him, his eyes opened, and they were the most radiant, reptilian blue that you can imagine. He bent his neck backward and continued to stretch—and as he stretched, he began to grow. His growth was quick. In just moments, he had gone from a small furry red ball to a height of more than thirteen feet. His soft fur had turned into scales that in another few moments hardened.

With anger and malice in his eyes, he looked down at the sleeping figure. Silently he moved next to Garen's side, and then with all of his fury—he struck. He grabbed Garen's arm with his talon. Instantly Garen awoke in agony as the dragon lifted him off of the ground by his arm, shook him, then threw him against the rock where he had slept.

"Going to kill dragons, are we?" he growled at Garen. "You haven't the power." He snarled as he, again and again, smashed Garen against the rock. You could hear the bones in Garen's arm break.

"Going to follow the King's command, are we? You fool. There are none greater than me! I am King of this world."

Letting go of Garen's mangled arm, the dragon reached his arms towards the sky. "I am the King of this world!" He screamed. "It belongs to me, and I claim it!"

But Garen remembered, "—the orb!"

With his arm in agony, and with every ounce of strength that he possessed, he reached for the pack which only moments before had been his pillow. There was no time to lose. He reached in and grabbed the small bundle that encased the orb. But before he could untie it, the dragon smashed his foot down upon Garen's back pinning him to the ground.

Garen cried out, "Almighty God—" But before he could say another word, the dragon smashed his foot once again into Garen's back.

As his ribs cracked, Garen screamed out in pain, "Almighty—save me!"

The dragon snarled, "No one will save—"

But before he could even finish the words that were on his tongue, the orb came bursting out of the bundle—a brilliant white light glowing with power and authority and a life of its own.

It instantly smashed into the side of the dragon again and again as if some great

CAMPFIRE

sword being wielded by a great skilled warrior.

The dragon screamed in anger as he was buffeted by some invisible host. His talons were flailing trying to stop the orb's repeated strikes.

And then the dragon toppled to the ground just feet from where Garen lay. Garen, holding his arm against his side and in great pain cried out, "I trusted you! You were my friend. You were just a little—" but Garen's word died out.

"There are no little dragon's" snarled the dying beast. "We are all mighty!"

In another moment, there was silence. The orb came to rest next to Garen's side. Garen bandaged his arm tightly against his chest, and at first morning's light began to make his way down the mountain toward the kingdom in search of help.

APPENDIX

Themes and Key Verses

Story Adaptations

Learning A Story

Storytelling Techniques

Best Practices

A Story's End

APPENDIX

THEMES AND KEY VERSES

The Story of the Torch — 11
Themes: Witness, Evangelism, Disciple-making, Integrity
Key Verses: Matt. 28:19-20, Col. 3:23

Run of the Arrow — 13
Themes: Dependence, Concern for Others, Sin
Key Verses: Phil. 2:4, Eph. 4:32

The Great Knight — 17
Themes: Pride, Selfishness, Repentance
Key Verses: James 4:10, Phil. 2:3, Prov. 28:13

My Son — 21
Themes: Relationship with Christ, Materialism
Key Verses: Matt. 6:19-21, Phil. 3:7

The Great Strong One — 23
Themes: Gospel, Sin, Sovereignty, Mercy, Grace
Key Verses: Col. 1:16-17, Heb. 4:16

Enough — 29
Themes: Sacrifice, Materialism
Key Verses: Rom. 12:1

City Without Water — 33
Themes: Relationship with God, Sin
Key Verses: Isa. 59:2

A Slave Set Free — 35
Themes: Freedom, Slavery, Grace
Key Verses: Gal. 5:1, John 8:36

The Mountain Stream — 39
Themes: Concern for Others, Gospel, Witness, Sin

Key Verses: Col. 2:6, 1 John 2:6

The Man on the Cross — 43
Themes: Sacrifice, Gospel

Key Verses: Matt. 27:54, Acts 2:2-4

Where is the Christian? — 49
Themes: Conviction

Key Verses: Eph. 6:13, Matt. 5:10

El Capitan — 53
Themes: Sacrifice, Trust, Faith

Key Verses: Heb. 9:28, 10:14

The Lucky Stone — 57
Themes: Selfishness, Submission to God, Surrender

Key Verses: Luke 9:23, Pro. 3:5-6

God's Garden — 61
Themes: Christian Life, Sin, Temptation, Forgiveness, Dependence

Key Verses: James 1:12, Psa. 1:1-3

The Crowning of the King — 71
Themes: Service, Selfishness, Grace

Key Verses: 1 John 2:17, John 12:26

Legend of the Cottonwoods — 75
Themes: Integrity, Responsibility

Key Verses: Pro. 10:9, 1 Cor. 3:8, Luke 16:10

Forty Roman Wrestlers — 79
Themes: Conviction, Dedication, Witness

Key Verses: 1 Pet. 1:13, James 1:2-4

APPENDIX

The Blacksmith — 81
Themes: Sacrifice, Grace, Selflessness

Key Verses: Rom. 5:8, John 15:1

Goldie — 83
Themes: Temptation, Obedience

Key Verses: John 14:23, Matt. 26:41

Goosetown — 87
Themes: Gospel, Truth, Sin, Christian Life

Key Verses: James 1:22, Matt. 7:24, Phil. 4:13

Sir Brian's Shield — 89
Themes: Obedience, Integrity, Humility, Service

Key Verses: James 4:10, Pro. 21:3

Andy the Dragon Fighter — 95
Themes: Integrity, Obedience, Christian Life, Pride

Key Verses: James 1:19-25

The Widow's Son — 101
Themes: Providence, Truth

Key Verses: 1 Kings 17:7-24

New Rags For Old — 105
Themes: Sacrifice, Atonement, Gospel, Surrender

Key Verses: Matt. 11:28, 1 John 2:2

The Silver Orb — 109
Themes: Self-control, Temptation, Sin, "Be Killing Sin"

Key Verses: 1 Pet. 5:8-9

CAMPFIRE

STORY ADAPTATIONS

The Story of the Torch
• When opening the story, use communication examples that are relevant to your audience.

Run of the Arrow
• Consider using the phrase "Native American" instead of "Indian."

The Great Strong One
• See "Run of the Arrow"
• This story is part one of two. The second is "Enough." If telling them in one sitting, consider cutting the discussion about the forest, plain, sky, etc. and go right into the part concerning the worm in the leaves.

Enough
• See "Run of the Arrow"

The Mountain Stream
• This story pairs well with a personal testimony about a close friend who turned away from God.

El Capitan
• This story can be considered graphic. If telling to a younger audience then you will need to tone down the depictions of blood or eliminate it.

God's Garden
• This story is very long. Consider breaking it into two parts ending part one with the line "It blocked the gate and even closed in around the pines and hemlocks that circled the log cottage."

Legend of the Cottonwoods
• See "Run of the Arrow"

Goldie
• This story has been modified from its original form in favor of a happy ending. The original story included a puppy "Lucky" who remained obedient to the master. It also ended with Goldie's death as she was never found in the woods.

APPENDIX

LEARNING A STORY

Ways To Learn Your Story
Try reading your story over and over again. Meditate on it throughout the day. It might help to type or write it out. Draw a story chart. Some people prefer to just start telling it at once.

Memorization
Parts of the story can be memorized word for word such as beautiful beginnings and endings, important dialog, colorful expressions, rhymes, or repeated phrases. Don't try to memorize an entire story that way. Strict reciting creates a distance from your listeners that is hard to bridge.

Picture The Story
Imagine the scenes in your mind as clearly as possible. These images will help you recreate your story later as you tell it in front of your audience, whether you consciously recall them or not. Meet the characters. What do you think they look like? What are their names? How do they sound? How do they move? Watch the action in the story. Actually hear their conversations. Before you tell a story to someone, mentally witness the events yourself. After you have done that, you can relate them to your audience. Even if the story is fiction, think of it as if it happened and you were there.

Mirrors
It is beneficial to practice your story with a mirror. This can be an actual mirror, an audio/video recorder, or a friend. The mirror will help you know how you are doing.

Absorb The Story
It should become second nature. Your goal is to internalize the storyline. The version you tell won't convey everything from the original story, but it has to make sense. Once you have the storyline down, focus on how you tell it.

STORYTELLING TECHNIQUES

Repetition
Stories usually repeat important events three times. You should pay special attention to repeated phrases or rhymes. Repetition helps your listeners follow the story by providing specific landmarks.

Variety
With repetition, it is also important to use variety. Change your voice's tone, pitch, volume, speed, rhythm, and articulation. You can even use pauses. Variety catches the audience's attention.

Body Language
Use gestures but only as they help the story. Act out some of the actions and make them BIG. Gestures keep the audience's eyes on you. When two characters are in a conversation, try using cross-focus. Position the characters at opposing 45-degree angles. This will allow the audience to follow the conversation visually.

Pay attention to how you portray your characters. Give them existence through facial expressions, voice, posture, and gestures.

Your body is your instrument
Project your voice and sustain it throughout your story. To do this, make sure you are breathing deeply and correctly. To do this, place your hand on your stomach and inhale. You should feel your stomach push out as your lungs expand. Many people do the opposite, holding their stomachs and expanding their chests. Keep your back straight so that your lungs can fully expand.

Don't push your voice too hard or use it unnaturally (unless for a specific voice). Relax your throat and jaw along with the rest of your body. Try letting out a long sigh or the lion's yawn by opening your mouth wide and sticking out your tongue as far as possible.

Beginnings and Endings
Pay special attention to the way a story starts and ends. You may want to memorize an introduction to go along with your story. If speaking to a younger audience, try presenting your moral or purpose at the beginning so they know what to look for as the story is told.

APPENDIX

Also, your audience should be aware of when your story ends without you having to tell them it is. A good way of doing this is slowing down and emphasizing your words such as "happily ever after," "that's the end of that," or "and they never saw him again."

BEST PRACTICES

Check Your Space

Try to create an environment that is comfortable, intimate, and free from distractions. Look at your space ahead to spot problems and arrange any special needs, a stool, or a glass of water. Try to have time beforehand to collect yourself or to warm up your body and voice.

Make It Personal

Give your listeners everything you've got. Project your words to the back row so that everyone can hear you. Avoid using filler words like "um" or "y'know." Face your audience squarely and with a straight back. Avoid fidgeting, putting your hands in your pockets, or bouncing from foot to foot.

Make a personal connection with your listeners. Talk to them, not at them, and don't be afraid to talk with them. Try to make eye contact with your audience. If you have difficulty scanning all of them, focus mainly on the first row. If some aren't paying attention, focus on the ones who are.

Pace Yourself

As you tell your story, allow your listeners to see the story, time to laugh, feel, reflect, and hang on the edge of their seats for what comes next. It's easy to go too fast and hard to go too slow. If you are losing your audience's attention, try slowing down.

Be Interactive

As your audience responds to your story, allow your story to respond to your listeners. Make your voice and gestures bigger or smaller. Stretch or shrink parts of the story, paying attention to what works and what doesn't so that you can add or subtract next time.

APPENDIX

A STORY'S END

A good story captivates the audience, but a great story leaves them with a deep truth to consider long after the fire has burned out. Not every story's message is self-evident, and it is often necessary to explain its meaning.

Strong applications are firmly rooted in God's Word. It is tempting to simply slap a related verse to the end of a story and close in prayer. A storyteller aims to convey a compelling story and communicate biblical truth.

To deliver a conclusion that makes an impact, include these elements:

1. State the "Takeaway"
Each story should have one main takeaway point that the audience will consider. This is the moral or lesson that you are trying to illustrate. Take time to craft a simple and memorable way to say it. Remember to pull this truth out from Scripture.

2. Relate Common Needs
A great way to help deliver your takeaway is to describe common needs. This will connect your audience to the message. You can start with a personal example of how the lesson addresses a need in your life, then consider the needs of your audience.

3. Read God's Word
Internalize the verse and hold your Bible while reading it to your audience. Consider having an audience member read it for you (make sure you ask them in advance!) When introducing the passage, state your reference at least twice at the beginning and then again afterward. One goal should be that your audience will meditate on the verse independently.

One mistake beginner storytellers make is to improvise an ending. What a shame it is when a story falls flat due to an under-prepared application. Try writing out your conclusion and even a closing prayer.